Van

W9-BSX-362

THE BOGUS BUDDHA

Books by the Same Author

THE
BOGUS
BUDDHA

A Superintendent Otani Mystery

James Melville

Charles Scribner's Sons
New York

Collier Macmillan Canada
Toronto

Maxwell Macmillan International
New York Oxford Singapore Sydney

Mel

Charles Scribner's Sons
Macmillan Publishing Company
866 Third Avenue
New York, NY 10022

Collier Macmillan Canada, Inc.
1200 Eglinton Avenue East, Suite 200
Don Mills, Ontario M3C 3N1

This is a work of fiction. Names, characters, places, and incidents
either are the product of the author's imagination or are used ficti-
tiously. Any resemblance to events or persons, living or dead, is
entirely coincidental.

Library of Congress Cataloging-in-Publication Data

Melville, James.
    The bogus Buddha: a superintendent Otani mystery/James
Melville.
      p. cm.
    ISBN 0-684-19247-0
    I. Title.
PR6063.E439B64   1991
    823'.914—dc20   90-48629

10 9 8 7 6 5 4 3 2 1

Printed in the United States of America

To Carole Rawcliffe

Author's Note

Hyogo is a real prefecture, and its police force is the fifth largest in Japan. It is currently under the command of Superintendent Supervisor Takaji Kunimatsu, its Director General. I recently had the honour and pleasure of meeting Director General Kunimatsu and one of his senior colleagues, Senior Superintendent Kaoru Okada, in charge of criminal investigation work. These gentlemen not only welcomed me and entertained me most hospitably, but also were good enough to express a kindly interest in the doings of their fictional counterparts. Director General Kunimatsu knows better than anyone else that my characters are the product of my imagination. In expressing my grateful thanks to him and his colleagues, I must however make it clear that my respect for the many thousands of men and women who inhabit the real world of police work in Hyogo is both great and sincere.

James Melville, Kobe, March, 1990

The Japanese version of the title reads
Ganbutsu (False Buddha)

THE BOGUS BUDDHA

One

'Here, give the wretched things to me,' Superintendent Tetsuo Otani said. He had noticed a look of mounting panic in his wife's face as half a dozen deer shoved and jostled her, reaching for the flat biscuits she was trying to distribute among them. 'Quickly, before they mess up your clothes.'

Hanae handed the biscuits over with ill-disguised relief and Otani moved off, drawing the animals away from her; but she remained interested in the proceedings.

'That sweet little one isn't getting any. Over there, on your right. She looks so sad.'

'That sweet little one will do quite well one way or another on a day like today. They're all grossly overfed, if you ask me.'

Otani rapidly broke up and got rid of the deer-cakes he had bought at Hanae's insistence from one of the old women lined up in wait for the tourists as they arrived at Nara Park by bus, by taxi or on foot from Nara Station half a mile away. The famous deer that roamed freely in the park were unafraid of people, not so much tame as pushy, the adults among them strong, heavy and far from cute at close quarters. Children squealed with pleasure at first sight of them, but only the bolder spirits braved their approaches for more than a few seconds before thinking better of it.

Tossing the last few pieces of biscuit away and brushing the crumbs from his hands, Otani extricated himself from the importunate deer by means of a series of neat side-steps and rejoined Hanae. Then they set off in the direction of the

Todaiji temple and its majestic image of the Buddha, but slowly, because it was blisteringly hot that August Sunday. Hanae had, in spite of mutinous mumblings on his part, persuaded Otani to wear his natty new linen blazer with his crisp open shirt and lightweight slacks, while she looked every inch the comfortably-off wife of a senior official in a long-sleeved navy-blue silk dress with tiny white polka-dots, a wide-brimmed white hat and high-heeled shoes. The two ensembles – plus Hanae's very grand silk parasol – had made a sizeable dent in Otani's midsummer bonus, but these days they could well afford their innocent extravagances.

'Are you really sure you want to go round the Todaiji first? In those shoes?'

'Yes. We've plenty of time.'

'Very well, then. We'll take a taxi to the hotel afterwards. Cool off a bit before Her Ladyship arrives. I still can't see why we had to dress up just for Michiko's benefit. In this outfit I feel as if I ought to be carrying the flag in front of our Olympic team. And she'll very likely turn up in that weird grey thing that looks like a tent with holes in it.'

Hanae tightened her lips before replying. The fact that she was already regretting the high heels and beginning to realise that she had underestimated the distances involved made her all the more nettled.

'I do wish you wouldn't always be so rude about my little sister. For your information, the dress Michiko was wearing last time she visited us was sage green, not grey. It also happened to be an Issey Miyake original that must have cost her at least a month's salary. And it did *not* look like a tent with holes in it.'

Otani cast a sideways look at her and judged it wise to hold his peace for the moment. A few seconds later he was rewarded when Hanae stopped short and he saw that she was trying hard not to giggle.

'Oh dear, now I won't be able to keep a straight face if she is wearing it today. It was lovely, but it didn't really suit her all that well, I must admit. All the same, do try to be nice to her, won't you?'

'Of course I will. Actually I'm rather proud of having a full professor for a sister-in-law. And it's me she wants to talk to, it seems. Flattering.'

'That's what she said, yes.'

They walked on a little further, each thinking about Michiko Yanagida. She was a good ten years younger than Hanae, and had done very well indeed to achieve while still in her early forties the title of Professor of History at one of the most distinguished women's universities in Japan. That had been a few months earlier, with effect from the beginning of the academic year in April, and involved a move to Nara from Kyoto where she had previously been teaching.

Otani broke the silence, taking a paper handkerchief from his pocket and dabbing at his forehead with it. 'But she didn't say what about.'

'No. She was ringing from a payphone outside a shop in the village. She might have had somebody with her, I suppose. Um . . .'

'Yes?'

'I . . . I think I've changed my mind. Let's give the Todaiji a miss today after all, shall we? It *is* awfully hot. And Michiko's always early. She might even be there already.'

About fifteen minutes later their taxi drew up with a flourish outside the stately portico of the Nara Hotel. Having been paid, the driver operated the automatic door opener and Otani clambered out, glancing round appreciatively while Hanae was emerging more decorously. Meantime another taxi arrived and disgorged a dapper little man with a face like a monkey who paused for a moment on the steps and then bolted inside the building in apparent agitation.

'Now this is what I *call* a hotel,' Otani said with satisfaction

3

when Hanae joined him and the two taxis had disappeared in a flurry of gravel. 'I certainly can't complain about Michiko's choice of meeting place.'

Hanae said nothing. In fact she had herself specified the rambling, century-old two-storey Nara Hotel, knowing that it was very much to his conservative taste.

'I mean, just look at it. The entrance puts me in mind of the sort of temple that shoguns or daimyos used to retire to in the old days when they'd had enough of the rough and tumble of politics.'

Hanae smiled. 'And decided to run things from behind the scenes instead, you mean. It was originally built for foreigners, surely. When we used to think they were all giants. That's why the rooms are so huge . . .' Her voice trailed off as she realised that Otani was not paying attention, but watching a black-jacketed young man with the look of an assistant manager about him, who came outside holding a pad of cloth and went over to the glossy black announcement board placed to one side of the porch. On it the names of those hosting private parties that day and of the banqueting rooms reserved for them were painted in white.

Having become long-sighted over the past few years, from four or five yards away Otani could read that one of the bookings was for a wedding reception, and one for a reunion of the 1963 graduates of Nara senior high school. These were obviously the big affairs of the day, the remaining three being unspecified apart from a single name each, suggesting smaller private lunches. The calligraphy was better than average and Otani had a keen eye for such touches; but what interested him much more was that the hotel employee looked embarrassed, and that he was carefully expunging one of the three names. Soon enough the young man went back inside, and Otani turned back to Hanae.

'Well, let's go in, shall we?'

As one of the very few people in the world who could

4

usually interpret her husband's expression, Hanae was not to be fobbed off as easily as that. As they mounted the steps she looked at the names left on the board herself, but they meant nothing to her.

'Something caught your eye? Do you recognise any of the names?'

'Not exactly. I was just curious when that young fellow rubbed one out. A bit late to cancel a party on the day, surely?' He glanced at his watch. 'Even if it is only just gone twenty past ten. We have well over half an hour in hand, you know. I shouldn't think even Michiko's likely to show up for at least ten minutes or so.'

Accepting that her curiosity was going to remain unsatisfied at least for the time being, Hanae followed him into the spacious lobby where they separated, agreeing to find each other in the terrace coffee lounge at about a quarter to eleven. Hanae made for the ladies' room, leaving Otani wondering quite what was going to take her nearly twenty minutes; but on the other hand pleased to have a short breathing space before their meeting with Michiko.

He decided to use the time to try to find out whether or not the luncheon party planned for twelve noon in the Bamboo Room had in fact been cancelled at extremely short notice. He also wanted very much to know a little more about the person whose name had been deleted from the list beside the hotel porch. Keizo Hosoda was an ordinary enough sort of name which might well be borne by a good many men up and down Japan, but Otani knew of only one, and that particular Hosoda had been referred to in discussion in his office quite recently.

He therefore made his unobtrusive way to the banqueting wing, along a broad corridor alive with the bustle of hotel staff at work preparing for the expected influx of guests. Each of the suites and smaller dining rooms the corridor served was elegantly labelled, and the doors of many of them were propped open for ease of access. Making space for a shirtsleeved waiter propelling a trolley loaded with plates and trays of cutlery, Otani sidled for a moment into the Jewel Room, which was evidently reserved for the high school reunion.

It looked as if at least fifty or so middle-aged former schoolmates were attached enough to their *alma mater* to have signed up for the get-together. Waitresses were laying tables, and a technician was tapping a microphone on a dais at the far end, producing hollow thuds from the speakers and then, suddenly, an ear-splitting howl. Otani winced, withdrew and moved on, past the Plum and Pine Rooms and round a corner into a quieter backwater leading to men's and women's restrooms and to a bank of three pay-phones. Diagonally across from these he found the Bamboo Room.

Its doors were open too, revealing a pleasantly proportioned interior big enough to accommodate comfortably up to a couple of dozen seated guests. Peeping inside, Otani satisfied himself that the room was deserted and noted that the single long table was set for twelve. Then he thought he heard voices, and quickly moved across to one of the telephones, taking out his pocket diary as he did so. People were definitely approaching, but he had his diary open with the receiver in one hand and was feeding a few ten-yen pieces into the slot with the other by the time a man and a woman rounded the corner and went into the Bamboo Room.

Without turning his head, Otani was able to recognise out of the corner of his eye the monkey-faced little man who had arrived at the hotel immediately after himself and Hanae, and to see that he looked angry and upset. Otani was not particularly surprised. The disappearance of Keizo Hosoda's name from the board had followed too quickly after the new arrival saw it and rushed into the hotel for there to be much doubt that it was he who had ordered it to be erased. It was clear from what his companion – clearly a

6

member of the hotel's managerial staff – was saying that they were continuing a discussion begun in the manager's private office.

Having loudly asked the recorded weather information service if Suzuki-san was at home and waited for half a minute, Otani embarked on a conversation with an imaginary golf partner. This involved his asking terse questions about the details of a forthcoming visit to Karuizawa, interspersed with long pauses while the non-existent but nevertheless apparently slow-witted Suzuki replied at length. The doors of the Bamboo Room remained open, and by shifting his position as naturally as possible from time to time during the performance, Otani had ample opportunity to keep an eye on the pair.

It soon became obvious to him that the smartly turned-out hotel representative was not allowing herself to be in the least intimidated, but was nevertheless doing an admirably professional job of calming the man down. They began to move about the room, and after scrutinising the place-cards the man switched the positions of two of them. Otani was confirmed in his interpretation of the situation. The Hosoda luncheon was going ahead, but its organiser, whoever he was, wanted the occasion to go unnoticed by casual visitors to the hotel.

After loudly saying goodbye to the recorded weather forecast, Otani put the phone down and slipped into the adjacent men's room, half expecting monkey-face to pop in there too when he had finished checking the Bamboo Room arrangements. After taking the opportunity to make use of the lavish facilities provided, Otani therefore positioned himself just inside the closed door, quite ready to give the impression of being in the act of leaving should it be opened. It was not. Instead, he again heard the voices of the people he had been observing, and this time they were going, not coming.

He gave them time to round the corner of the corridor

and then went out of the men's room. There was nobody in sight, but the doors of the Bamboo Room had been closed. Otani hesitated for no more than a few moments before deciding that the risk of being spotted was minimal if he were to take a quick look inside. Seconds later he was walking round the table jotting into his diary the names on the place-cards. The corridor was still deserted when he had finished and peeped outside, and within a short time he was sauntering into the terrace lounge in high good humour.

Hanae and Michiko were already there, at a table for four overlooking the garden with its pleasant Japanese touches: a stone lantern, a miniature bridge with red-lacquered rails not much more than a foot high. The two women had their backs to him, so Otani paused in the doorway and surveyed the scene before going over to join them.

The terrace lounge waitresses were being kept busy by what looked like very nearly a capacity crowd of people of every age and sort. At least a dozen of them, ranged round three neighbouring tables, were obviously wedding guests filling in time before the reception. The women were dressed up in formal kimonos which down to about knee level were in plain black, relieved only at the neck by the edges of their white undergarments, and on their backs by the white embroidered crests of their families. Below the knee it was a different story, for the hems and lower parts of their kimonos were richly decorated with great splashes of gold, red and other bold colours.

All but one of their menfolk wore black jackets with striped trousers – undertaker costume except for their neckties which were grey or silver. The exception was a youngish man, resplendent in much the same colour scheme but in the full Japanese rig of *hakama* and *haori* – the stiff, full length divided skirt with kimono-style top and over it a short loose jacket of heavy silk secured across his chest by a splendid woven cord and tassel. On his feet were *tabi* socks with a separate compartment for the big toe and flat sandals of fine straw, and he looked altogether pleased with himself. Indeed, when a western tourist approached him, egged on by her woman companion, and with questioningly raised eyebrows and a timid smile pointed at her camera, the man not only nodded agreement but graciously stood up so that she might photograph him full length.

A noisy party of three men and three women to Otani's right constituted a sharp contrast. The women were also done up to the nines in kimonos, but theirs were gaudy, and worn more loosely at the neck than those of the respectable bourgeois ladies of the wedding party. This spirited trio looked to Otani as if they were a lot nearer forty than thirty but not in the least bit sorry about it; nicely run in, as it were, but with a lot of useful mileage to look forward to. In other words, ideal companions for their three middle-aged escorts, heavy-set men whose colourful Hawaiian sports shirts were strained across their fleshy chests, and who appeared to have more than their fair share of solid gold teeth and matching wristwatches between them.

Amused by their uproarious good humour, Otani picked his way among the tables, with a good view of Michiko's profile as he drew nearer to her. She was talking animatedly to Hanae, and Otani's first impression was that whatever it was that had prompted her to ask specifically to see him, she was certainly not in any apparent distress. Nor, thank goodness, was she wearing the dress he had been rude about, but what to him was an unremarkable but presumably expensive product of the couturier's art. Her hair-style too was different. The unnatural frizzy mop she had affected during her Kyoto years had been replaced by a simple, softer arrangement, which made Otani notice for the first time that Michiko had unusually large and attractive eyes for a Japanese woman.

'Good morning,' he said politely when he was near enough to their table for the two sisters to notice him. 'Sorry I'm a bit late. You did well to find such a good table. Well,

Michiko. You look very nice if I may say so.' He slipped into the vacant chair next to her, meeting the look of wary suspicion she flashed at him with a benign smile.

'Good morning. Are you actually paying me a *compliment*?'

'I am indeed.'

'Well, thank you. Forgive my reaction, but it's a new experience. I'm glad you approve of them.'

Hanae was quick to interpret the blank look on her husband's face and come to his rescue. 'I'm thinking about getting some contact lenses myself, now that I'm beginning to need my glasses more often than not. Mi-chan says the new kind are hardly any bother.'

Having been flushed with his recent success in the Bamboo Room, Otani was shocked to realise that he had failed such an elementary test of his powers of observation when it came to his own wife's sister. Fortunately at that moment a waitress came to take their order and the interlude gave him time to compose himself.

After the girl returned with coffee and strawberry cheese-cake for three, the subject of contact lenses was finally laid to rest, and Michiko began to explain what was bothering her.

Two

Keizo Hosoda belched, snapped his fingers loudly and pointed at the side table. On it were open bottles of Chivas Regal Scotch whisky, Hine VSOP cognac and Gordon's gin, with a bucket of ice and ample supplies of tonic and soda water. Hosoda had no need to speak – three junior guests at once scrambled from their seats, two of them reached his side almost simultaneously, and the one who actually secured the great man's glass and took it over to refresh his drink did so with an expression of frozen dedication on his face.

From his seat near the double doors, Zenji Ono kept a watchful eye on the proceedings but permitted himself to judge that everything seemed to be going swimmingly in the Bamboo Room. Coffee had been served, the table largely cleared and the waiters dismissed. The assembled company had feasted off hors d'oeuvres followed by cold lobster with salad, Kobe beef steaks and strawberries with cream, and the meal – he had as a matter of course chosen the most expensive of the four set menus offered by the Nara Hotel – had apparently given satisfaction to the three men present who mattered. Ono had no interest in the reactions of the rest. Thank heavens he had been able to get that name deleted from the notice board outside, well before any of the others turned up.

He realised now that he had made an error of judgment in instructing the banquet manager to have place-cards prepared, and wished he hadn't bothered. Some of the lesser

11

lights among the guests had clearly been gratified to see their names on display, and unused to being so honoured had already pocketed their cards as souvenirs of the occasion; but the grandees seemed barely to have noticed them, and the whole silly contretemps earlier could and should have been avoided. Keizo Hosoda's name was one to be conjured with, but nowadays only in certain carefully restricted circles. It had obviously meant nothing to the hotel manager to whom Ono had protested. The manager had ordered its removal with no more than a barely concealed shrug; and the composed young woman who had subsequently escorted Ono to the Bamboo Room to check the arrangements was clearly of the unspoken opinion that he had been making a great fuss about nothing.

It was simply that Hosoda-san's name had been at the top of the list provided, she explained. They had therefore assumed that he was the guest of honour, and followed their usual practice in putting it on the board; but if all those attending the lunch had already been advised that it was to take place in the Bamboo Room she agreed that there was no need to announce the fact.

Perhaps he had overreacted, but one could never be too careful where Keizo Hosoda was concerned. Hosoda was imperious and high-handed: the way he had got his drink refreshed was characteristic. His anger could be as terrifying as it was unpredictable. On the other hand he could switch on a disarming charm of manner. Ono had been watching him working on the men seated to his right and left, attending graciously to each of them in equal turns. He was now treating the whole company to an indulgent smile, looking from side to side while lumbering to his feet glass in hand.

'Listen, everybody. I have one or two things to say, now that we've all enjoyed the good food and drink arranged for us by my old friend Ono-kun over there. Yes, that's him over there by the door, the one staring at the tablecloth and trying not to look embarrassed. Now to begin with, I'll let you in on a big secret. I'm not the only one with something to celebrate today. It's Ono's birthday – so everybody except him, up on your feet and we'll sing "Happy Birthday". All together, now . . .'

Absurdly, Ono felt a prickling at the back of his eyes during the twenty seconds or so it took the others to get through the English jingle in ragged chorus. Hosoda was an extraordinary man. Fancy his remembering a triviality like that, when with so much on his mind the birthday boy himself had quite forgotten that he was fifty-two that day!

'Yes, I've known Ono-kun since we were kids together just after the war,' Hosoda was rambling on in reminiscent vein. 'And I remember his birthday because we were working the black market together. Down in Kobe, under the railway arches. We had a good little operation going, didn't we, Ono? Running errands between dealers who wanted to trade with each other in a hurry to suit particular customers. Cartons of Camels or Lucky Strikes for nylons or whisky, that sort of thing, and a couple of cigarettes or a pack of American gum for our trouble each time. Worth very good money. You'd be surprised how the takings mounted up.' Several of the men seated round the table were obviously under thirty, and Hosoda paused to eye each of them.

'You youngsters don't have a clue what I'm on about, do you? Never mind. Anyway, the summer of forty-seven or forty-eight it must have been, we were nabbed by a couple of cops. First time it had happened to us. I was ready to make a bolt for it, but Ono didn't turn a hair. Just looked up at them as cool as you like and said not today, mister, not on the tenth of August. Oh, and what's so special about the tenth of August, the cop wants to know. It's my birthday, that's what, says Ono. And a special one. Lucky double ten. I'm ten years old today. So we'll just be getting along. And that's exactly what we did. They were so tickled by his cheek they just stood there and watched us vamoose . . .'

As Hosoda went on about the hard, good old days of their shared youth, Ono watched the other men round the table pretending to hang on his words. The seniors managed an occasional indulgent smile; the juniors contributed frequent bursts of forced, sycophantic laughter. His old associate's story had jogged Ono's memory, and he now recalled their encounter with the two policemen. It was not the first time he had managed to talk himself and Hosoda out of trouble, nor the last by any means, for their paths had crossed and re-crossed over the decades.

Not that they had remained in business together for very long as boys. In 1949 Zenji Ono's father was repatriated from the Soviet Union where he had been a prisoner of war, and after a period of convalescence returned to the school-teaching career he had barely embarked on before being conscripted. Horrified when he discovered the extent to which young Zenji had been allowed to run wild by his distracted mother, he took the boy in hand. Within a matter of months Zenji's native intelligence and quick wit had been effectively harnessed to school work, and he became a star pupil. A couple of years later he passed easily into one of the new-style junior high schools, and by the time his father died while still in his forties Zenji had finished with senior high school too and was a law student at Osaka University.

It wasn't until he was twenty-four and a newly qualified attorney that Ono met Keizo Hosoda again. Ono had recently joined one of the bigger law offices in Kobe. He owed his job to one of the professors at Osaka University, who had failed to persuade Ono to attempt the civil service examinations but nevertheless continued to take a kindly interest in the young man's future. Stepping out of his office building one day on his way to a late lunch, Ono had been taken aback to be accosted by a big, heavily built man in a flashy suit who clapped him on the shoulder in a friendly way.

Two hours later Ono had a stack of crisp new five-thousand yen notes half a centimetre thick in his inside pocket, an informal side job as confidential legal adviser to his boyhood friend, and a surprised respect for Hosoda's powers of persuasion. Hosoda had made it his business to keep himself informed about Ono's school and university career, but was not forthcoming about the way in which he had himself spent the past twelve or thirteen years. Ono was not naive. It was obvious to him that Hosoda – involved in what he referred to as 'various enterprises, this and that, you know' – had become some sort of gangster, and the prospect of being covertly associated with him had a piquant appeal. The handsome initial retainer and the promise of easy money to come enhanced it.

In his regular job Ono was concerned with company law, a fact that Hosoda had of course discovered before approaching him. Within six months Ono had helped Hosoda to set up his first independent enterprise: an employment agency. Hosoda's own name appeared no-where in the legal documentation: he produced nominees to 'act' as president, company secretary and treasurer. Ono presumed they were either related to Hosoda in some way or were underworld associates, but learned very soon that it didn't do to be too inquisitive about Hosoda's connections.

Three more companies came into existence during the next two years, and then Ono resigned from the law office in order to become the genuine and acknowledged executive director and secretary of the fourth, which they called Elite Property Developments. Its board of non-executive directors was again composed of nonentities, and never met. By then Ono was well aware that the so-called employment agency procured women to work out of bars and in bath-houses as prostitutes, that the public relations agency was the base for a protection and blackmailing racket, and that the publishing company produced *biniru*, pornographic magazines sealed in transparent plastic covers to frustrate would-be browsers.

By contrast, the bona fides of Elite Property Developments were legally impeccable. In spite of the very high salary Hosoda paid him, Ono would not have agreed to run the company were it otherwise. Hosoda kept his name out of it, but he and Ono had a gentleman's agreement securing for Hosoda the lion's share of the profits. Elite Property Developments prospered mightily and legitimately in the boom years of the sixties. Indeed, within a few years they were making so much money out of speculation in land that Ono began to resent the time he had to devote behind the scenes to sorting out the legal tangles into which Hosoda's sleazier enterprises landed themselves whenever the police decided to pounce.

They met only when Hosoda summoned him, usually to the lobby of a de luxe hotel in Kobe, Osaka, Nagoya or even sometimes Tokyo. Often on these occasions Ono tried to persuade him that the time had come to divest himself of the embarrassing and potentially troublesome parts of his business empire, but with complete lack of success. Hosoda reacted either with patient indulgence, explaining that he valued all his associates and had no intention of letting them down, or with one of the terrifying outbursts of anger that still, after many years experience of them, left Ono white-faced and trembling. Eventually Ono gave up, deciding that Hosoda quite simply enjoyed being on the wrong side of the law – and realising at the same time that in his heart of hearts he admired him for it.

Making very sure that he was personally at all times legally unassailable, Ono continued to run Elite Property Developments with flair and efficiency; and without cheating Hosoda in any way. Hosoda had, after all, put up the initial capital; and in any case enough of the profits came Ono's way for him to have built up a substantial fortune for himself. At the same time he gave Hosoda disinterested legal advice whenever asked for it, but shied away from involvement in the creation of any more new companies. That Hosoda found others to act for him in that context soon became clear to Ono, for whom it became something of a hobby to detect Hosoda's hand in dubious financial operations of one sort and another.

The man himself seemed to enjoy a charmed life – until his current live-in mistress embarked on an affair with a television actor. When Hosoda found out, he promptly, personally and publicly – in Osaka – shot and seriously injured the actor, and was equally promptly arrested and charged. On conviction he faced up to ten years in prison for causing bodily injury, and up to three for possession of a gun without authorisation. No lawyer in the country could have kept Hosoda out of prison, but Ono secured for him the services of the best specialist in criminal law in western Japan, who managed to persuade the court that a total of five years would meet the case.

Greatly to his surprise, no sooner had Hosoda been put out of circulation than Ono found himself being approached by emissaries on behalf of a man he knew to be a senior member of an organised crime syndicate, and who, it seemed, was most anxious to meet him. He thought very hard before agreeing to the proposal, and subsequently realised that by holding back he had strengthened his hand. When eventually he did call on the gangster boss who was now sitting on Hosoda's right looking bored and picking his teeth, Ono was treated with a wary respect, and inferred as the discussion proceeded that his hesitation had been mis-interpreted as the adoption of a tough and haughty bargaining posture.

For by the time that crucial conversation had run its roundabout and allusive course, Ono had been confirmed in his suspicion that while maintaining a very low personal profile Keizo Hosoda had for years functioned as financial adviser to the syndicate. He had learned also that Hosoda had appointed a representative and plenipotentiary to act on his behalf until his eventual release from jail, and that he, Ono, was to be that representative. That was the real surprise, and it took Ono some time to take it in, and to begin to appreciate both its implications and the extent of the powers which had been placed in his hands for a period of several years.

In the short term Ono kept his own counsel, made himself readily available to his new friends for consultation, and added a great deal of new material to his already impressive bank of information about Hosoda's activities and interests. As the months went by and he sensed that Hosoda's gangster associates were beginning not only to accept him but to value and depend on his advice, he began to plan new ventures. None of these could of course be referred to on paper, but Ono was able to drop hints when he visited Hosoda in the prison on the southern outskirts of Kyoto – not too often, because the shooting case had attracted a lot of publicity at the time and one or two of the papers had referred darkly to possible connections with organised crime. No reporter had sniffed out any link with Elite Property Developments, though, and Ono had no desire to draw attention to himself.

*

Ono was beginning to feel as restive as everybody else round the table seemed to be. Hosoda was going on too long, and trying people's patience. One had to make allowances for a man newly out of jail after five years, but enough was enough.

On the other hand, it was quite interesting to see how the experience of imprisonment had affected him; softened his edges somehow, inclined him to sentimentality. The cat who had so insistently walked alone, the secretive operator so jealous of his privacy, would never have agreed to appear at a festive meal in his honour. Yet during his final weeks in prison Hosoda had jumped at the idea, and himself suggested most of the names on the guest list. Ono knew who some of them were, of course, but had never heard of several. Having now met them, he wouldn't dream of inviting a single one of these associates of Hosoda to his own table.

All in all, Hosoda was certainly a man full of contradictions. He was – or had been – formidable and inventive, deft and ruthless in dealings, yet as trusting as a child in insisting on building his empire on legal sand. He seemed to hold some of the most unlikely and unappetising people in genuine regard, and as a consequence to have become something of a father figure to the younger and simpler of them.

Hosoda was now, at long last, winding up his speech, and Ono looked at him with a certain sympathy. It was in many ways rather a pity that he had to be killed.

Three

'Well, gentlemen. The main subject for confidential discussion today so far as I'm concerned is Keizo Hosoda.' The officers representing the administration, personnel and traffic sections at Hyogo Prefectural Police Headquarters had just trooped out of his shabby but spacious office at the end of the regular Tuesday morning briefing meeting, and Otani was left in the company of his three principal lieutenants. His own papers were still on the conference table, but Inspectors Kimura and Hara had taken theirs over to the smaller, low table they always sat round when Otani summoned his inner cabinet. Inspector Noguchi never had any papers anyway. 'When was it he was let out, Ninja?'

'Saturday morning. Five o'clock. Early because my oppo in Kyoto thought some of the lads might stage a bit of a welcome back show outside the jug, but it seems it was a bit of a damp squib.'

'Not really. The festivities were more select, and took place the following day. Sunday.' Otani gazed expressionlessly at his old friend, relishing the rare chance to upstage him in a matter concerning the underworld. The story went that Noguchi's nickname had in the distant past been bestowed on him by an outraged crook when he materialised apparently miraculously in a supposedly secret and secure hideaway in the middle of a payout ceremony involving serious money. Whether or not that was how he had come by the name, Noguchi's remarkable talent for melting into the background and emerging when and where least expected like the *ninja* of medieval Japan had, over the years, given him almost mythical status in the eyes of local professional criminals and his younger police colleagues alike. Otani knew it was too much to hope that Noguchi would express either surprise or chagrin on discovering that he was in this instance less well informed than his superior, but he did open both eyes at the same time, which was something he did very rarely when slumped in an easy chair.

Having savoured the attentive silence for a few seconds, Otani resumed.

'I have to admit that I came by this information quite by chance. My wife and I were in Nara on Sunday, and dropped in at the Nara Hotel. Ordinarily I don't suppose I'd have paid the slightest attention to the notice-board they put outside old-fashioned places like that, but something drew my attention to it.' Otani saw no reason at that stage to go into detail. 'Anyway, the list of private parties and so forth due to take place in the hotel that day included a lunch in honour of Keizo Hosoda.' He directed an enquiring look at Inspector Takeshi Hara, who had taken off his glasses and was blinking while he polished them. He was the only person Otani knew who invariably used the special little cloth provided by the optician for this purpose. 'Must be the same man, wouldn't you think?'

'Possibly, sir. I would hesitate to go further.'

'Quite right too. Not without better evidence. But let me just hark back to last week, when you were telling us about this so-called greenmailing business you've been looking into. You're all well aware I'm no financial expert, but as I understood you, it amounts to a variation on the old *sokaiya* game, where a few gangsters each buy a handful of shares in a company so as to have the right to attend the annual general meeting, and then threaten beforehand to break it up if they're not bought off. Used to, anyway, before the law was tightened up. Right?'

Hara pursed his lips briefly before replying. He hated loose analogies. 'Greenmailing is indeed a method of extortion from companies, but hardly comparable with the techniques of sokaiya who, with respect, sir, still exist.'

'Just go about it a bit less obviously, do they?'

'Precisely. Sokaiya nowadays tend indeed to be rather more subtle and polished than their thuggish predecessors of ten years ago, but essentially they still threaten their victims with physical action. Successful greenmailing involves nothing like that. Moreover, it calls for high intelligence and a flair for interpreting and predicting the movements of the stock market on the part of the instigator. The greenmailer – who must have substantial funds available at the outset – selects a company with excellent prospects. He legitimately acquires a substantial holding in it, and then persuades the management to buy the shares back through a confidential agent at an inflated price.'

'Yes, but how? I didn't follow that bit last time.'

Inspector Jiro Kimura had been scrutinising his cuticles, now and then pushing one back delicately with the thumbnail of the other hand. Now he desisted, looked up and answered for Hara. 'If the company doesn't play ball, the greenmailer threatens to unload his holding at giveaway prices and wreck public confidence in the firm.'

Hara looked pained at hearing the point put with such economy, but nodded his head in agreement.

'Ah, now I see. Now let me get this next bit right. You and Ninja think that Takeuchi's outfit here in Kobe have been going in for greenmailing in the last couple of years or so, right?'

'Sure of it,' Noguchi said from the depths of his chair. 'But Takeuchi knows as much about the stock market as I do about ballet dancing.'

'So he's being advised by somebody a lot better informed. An expert, in fact. Fair enough, but what makes you think it's Hosoda? Before he lost his head and shot that actor in

Osaka a few years ago I'd never heard of him. Had you, Ninja?'

Noguchi stirred in his chair. 'Vaguely. Picked up odds and ends of talk here and there. Never spotted him as a ranking member of the Takeuchi mob, true. He kept well out of sight as a rule. The tax people took a bit of an interest in him. They were pretty sure he got big money off Takeuchi, or that partner of his, Ikeda. But they never managed to find his name on any dodgy bits of paper.'

'So he's not a complete unknown. All right, if you and Hara think he's Takeuchi's freelance expert, I'll go along with you. All the same, that still leaves two questions that bother me. First, how has he managed to read the market so cleverly during the past couple of years when he's been in prison?'

Hara tried to be kind. 'Ah, that puzzled me too, sir. But then I realised that he would have had access to the newspapers and to television. So I consulted the prison warden by telephone. He kindly looked into the matter and later rang back to confirm that the warders reported that Hosoda diligently studied the daily financial press and weekly economic journals. Again, he might well have been visited and briefed by associates with specialised knowledge.'

Otani sighed. 'That's what I deserve for asking silly questions, I suppose. All right, see if you can shoot this one down as easily. If Hosoda is so smart, why doesn't he simply play the market openly like any other speculator and make an honest fortune, instead of going in with the likes of Takeuchi?'

The short silence that followed was broken by a prolonged gurgling noise, and everybody, including its owner, looked towards Noguchi's belly. 'Getting on for lunchtime,' he remarked, unabashed. 'Good question, that. My guess'd be it never occurred to him to do things the easy way. How come you were at the Nara Hotel anyway?'

Coming from either of the others the question would have been a gross impertinence, but Noguchi was the oldest man in the room, and the most senior inspector in the force. In Japan, exceptional privileges go with age and status, but there was even more to it than that. Otani's personal regard for his old crony was such that he permitted him familiarities often verging on the insolent.

All the same, he took his time over replying and made them all wait while he helped himself to another cup of cold green tea from the big thermos flask on the table. 'It had nothing to do with greenmailing, I can assure you. But I'd intended to pick your brains today about something else arising from my trip to Nara anyway, so I might as well do it now. My wife and I went there to see her sister.' He turned to Kimura, the muscles round his mouth twitching almost imperceptibly. 'You've met her. Seen her, anyway. Remember the fracas at that international student society party in Kyoto?'

'I'm not likely to forget it, or Professor Yanagida.'

'No, I suppose not. Well, she's teaching in Nara now, and still very internationally minded. It seems she's helping with some sort of summer school at the moment, involving both Japanese and *gaijin*. To do with Japanese culture. I wouldn't bother to mention it if it weren't for the fact that it's taking place in this prefecture. Well, most of it, anyway. Any of you ever heard of a temple called Anraku-in, in the country north-east of here, somewhere beyond Inagawa?'

Kimura was very possessive where foreigners were concerned, and his reaction was immediate and predictably huffy. 'An international summer school? In this prefecture? I can't imagine why my people didn't inform me. Did Professor Yanagida happen to mention how many foreigners are taking part?'

Beyond shaking his head at him almost imperceptibly Otani made no reply, but turned to Hara who had seemingly been seeking inspiration from the ceiling. 'Mean anything to you?'

Hara pronounced the name with deliberation, stressing the final syllable. 'Anraku-*in*. Curious. No, sir, I haven't heard of such a place before today. But that part of the prefecture is more or less due west of Kyoto. It sounds as if Sasayama would be the nearest sizeable town, and that can't be more than, oh, forty kilometres at most away. There is also a direct road link to Kyoto, I fancy. Now we know that the eminent priest Sakuden retired to a pavilion which he called Anraku-*an* after he ceased to be the abbot of Seigei-ji in Kyoto.'

Kimura looked at Hara sharply. 'When was this?'

'Oh, about three hundred and fifty years ago.'

Otani enjoyed the exchange. 'It seems you weren't informed of that either, Kimura-kun. Too bad. But then I must confess that neither was I. What about you, Ninja?'

The wheezing noise Noguchi was making suggested that he too was amused. 'Never heard of the place. Or this Sakuden guy,' he managed eventually.

'Enlighten us all, would you, Inspector?' Hara had been head of the criminal investigation section at Hyogo Prefectural Police Headquarters for long enough to have made his mark, and at last Otani was beginning to enjoy his pedantic style. Noguchi had – inexplicably to Otani – taken to the young man from Nagasaki from the first, and even Kimura, who hated being upstaged, nowadays grudgingly admitted that Hara knew his stuff.

'If I am right in inferring a connection with Sakuden, the organisers of the summer school under discussion made a happy choice of venue. Sakuden is remembered as a poet, a connoisseur of the tea ceremony, and a popular preacher and author of amusing stories. A good communicator, in short.'

Otani gazed at him in some awe, but Kimura pretended to be less impressed. 'And no doubt you also know what he did in his spare time.'

Hara smiled at him with singular sweetness. 'Yes. He grew camellias and wrote a book about them.'

Noguchi stirred in his chair. As always, this made everybody else sit up and pay attention to him. 'What's the trouble at this place, then?'

'Thank you, Ninja,' Otani said at once. 'For bringing us back to the point. That was all very interesting, but hardly relevant. I'll try to be brief. Kimura asked how many people are taking part in this summer school. I don't know, but from what my sister-in-law said I gathered that it was upwards of three dozen. Enough to fit into one fair-sized tour bus, anyway. About half of them are Japanese, and half of various other nationalities. For the first week or so they were all at Anraku-in. Then they went off on a conducted bus tour, visiting various important historic places – castles, temples, shrines, old burial mounds and so on. Famous craft centres, too. Potteries, she mentioned, a swordsmith, villages where they produce special kinds of cloth, all that kind of thing.' He helped himself to yet more tea, but pulled a face because it had become bitter.

'They were due back at the temple or whatever it is today, or maybe it was yesterday, for the final couple of weeks. My wife's sister's rejoining them there. She had to duck out of the tail end of the tour – some important faculty meeting or other at her new university. The thing is, she's not too happy about the way the summer school's going. A lot of tensions among some of the people involved.'

'That's hardly surprising,' Kimura put in. 'In my experience culture vultures are a quarrelsome lot. Um, I wasn't referring to Professor Yanagida, needless to say,' he added hastily.

27

'Nor to our erudite colleague Hara, I hope.' In the face of this unexpected compliment from his boss Hara gazed modestly at his knees. 'I take your point, though,' Otani went on imperturbably. 'However, I gather this isn't a matter simply of academic squabbles. Some disturbing things have happened, both at Anraku-in and on the tour, it seems. Including at least two mishaps, either of which might easily have had fatal consequences, and both endangering the same person. My sister-in-law – an imaginative but highly intelligent woman, by the way – isn't convinced they were accidents.'

Otani glanced at his watch, registered slight surprise and sat up straight. 'I'm sorry to have taken so long over this, and I realise that in all probability there's nothing whatever in it for us. All the same, it might be worth an informal sniff round the place and the people there. You'd better go yourself if you can spare the time, Kimura. Give your English a bit of an airing. Your French too, perhaps. You said you ought to have known about a bunch of gaijin at a summer school on our patch, anyway. Right, Ninja advised us some time ago it was nearly lunchtime. Thank you all.'

Otani, Kimura and Hara rose to their feet and waited for Noguchi to finish extricating himself with ponderous majesty from his own chair. The process completed, he confronted Otani.

'Quite sure it was our Hosoda at the Nara Hotel, are you?'

'I am now, yes. You see, Takeuchi and his partner Ikeda were down to attend the lunch too.' Otani produced his diary and handed Noguchi a leaf he tore out of it. 'I almost forgot to give you this. I jotted down the names of all twelve guests, thinking you might be interested. You and Hara will probably recognise some of the others. Now I really ought to be off. Excuse me if I leave you to it.'

Kimura got to the door first and held it open for Otani, who treated him to the merest suspicion of a smile. 'Enjoy your day in the country,' he said as he passed him. 'You never know, among the foreign women there might be one who's just your type.'

Four

'You know, you're a very interesting person.' Kimura bestowed his most roguish smile upon his companion, who raised her left eyebrow perhaps a millimetre in response. 'Right out here in the country and all, I certainly didn't expect to meet a British lady.'

'You're somewhat out of the ordinary yourself, Mr . . .'

'Kimura, Jiro Kimura.'

'Mr Kimura. I'm Philippa Kilpeck. You must be bored by having westerners compliment you on your English.'

'Oh, I don't know. When I tell people I was born and partly brought up in America they realise there's nothing special about it.'

'I see. All the same, it is impressive, if I may say so.'

As the bus swayed and rattled on along the dusty road, Kimura shifted in his seat, partly turning towards her. Eyes half closed, he sniffed delicately. 'Chanel number nineteen?'

'Well done.'

Emerging from Sasayama station with the intention of finding a taxi to take him to Anraku-in by taxi, Kimura had seen the foreign woman waiting alone at the nearby bus stop, and made the elementary deduction that she was in all probability one of the participants in the summer school. He was much impressed by the simple elegance of her appearance. The short-sleeved white cotton dress was held in at the waist by a red silk sash fastened at one hip; its colour perfectly matched by the band round the broad-brimmed hat that shadowed her face, her straw handbag and her sandals. A heavy gilded chain at her neck and gold earrings were her only jewellery. Never one to hesitate over breaking the ice where attractive women were concerned, he sauntered over and joined her, raising his own natty cream-coloured trilby-style sun hat with elaborate politeness, a cheery good morning and an appreciative remark about the weather. A bus was pulling into the station forecourt, and when it drew up at the stop and she boarded it he followed her, settling into the seat beside her as if they were old friends. This was not, he was well aware, altogether to her liking, but he kept the conversation going after a fashion with banalities to which she responded at first off-handedly.

After a while her manner thawed, and during the past few minutes she had been more forthcoming. Kimura had established that she was British, and that this was her first visit to Japan. After scrutinising her discreetly, he had decided that she was probably in her mid thirties, and noticed that there was no wedding ring among the several she was wearing on her long, slender fingers.

'Well, if I'm not being too inquisitive, what brings you to this out-of-the-way part of Japan, ah, Miss, or should I say Ms Kilpeck?'

'Doctor, actually.'

'*Doctor* Kilpeck? You're a doctor?'

She smiled. Her mouth was wide and generous, and Kimura thought she looked a little like Julie Christie, by whose charms in his younger days he had been greatly struck.

'Not a medical doctor. I'm a historian.'

'Is that right? By the way, excuse me for asking, but shouldn't that be *an* historian?'

'Some people still pronounce it in that way. Either will do.'

'That's interesting, you said "eether" like an American. I

thought "eyether" was correct British usage.'

Dr Kilpeck flung up her hands in a brief gesture of amused exasperation. 'You simply *have* to be a schoolmaster, Mr Kimura. Am I right?'

Kimura was shocked. 'Me, a teacher? No, ma'am. I'm . . . a journalist.' While still on the train he had wondered whether to turn up at the temple in the guise of an anonymous tourist or to represent himself as someone with a professional interest in what was going on there. Now the decision was made. He always carried a small selection of bogus name-cards, and could if necessary produce from the neat little bag dangling from his wrist one which would support his claim.

'Really? Which paper?'

'I'm a freelance. I'm not sure I'd like a regular job on a daily paper. The weekly magazines pay well, and they're a better prospect as far as I'm concerned. I'm taking a vacation just now, if you can call it that. Hence the camera. Going wherever the mood takes me, exploring parts of Hyogo Prefecture I haven't seen before. But the bills still have to be paid, so I'm always on the lookout for interesting people and stories. That's why I sort of forced my company on you. Sorry about that.'

'You're forgiven. At least you're the first Japanese I've met since I've been here who hasn't asked me if I can eat raw fish. I warn you, if you do I shall probably scream.'

'I won't. Promise. Where are you getting off, by the way?'

'At a place called Anraku-in. I'm attending a summer school there. It's the next stop, I think.'

Kimura looked towards the translucent destination panel at the front of the bus. It bore about a dozen place-names, and each, with the fare payable, was illuminated in turn as the bus progressed.

'Next but one. Sounds interesting. A summer school for historians?'

'No, it covers a number of subjects. Most of us are specialists of one sort or another but there are general lectures too.
They amount to an introductory course on the classical
Japanese arts and traditional crafts for those of us from
overseas. I had to go to the post office in the town, so I've
missed a talk on the incense ceremony, I'm afraid.'

'The incense ceremony? Doesn't mean very much to me,
I must admit. You know,' Kimura went on as if the thought
had just occurred to him, 'there could be a feature article in
this. Would you mind if I get off with you and drop in?
Have a word with the secretary or director or whatever and
ask permission to look around?'

Dr Kilpeck shrugged slightly, affording Kimura a brief
but pleasing glimpse down the front of her dress.

'No harm in asking, I suppose, if you've nothing better to
do. I'll show you where the summer school office is. The
secretary is a Miss Yasuda. You'd better ask for Professor
Kido. He's really in charge, but he has an American co-
director. Bill Ashley. Mr Ashley deals with administration,
and organises the lectures and demonstrations for those of
us who don't speak Japanese. Here we are.'

'I'll go first. No, no, put your purse away, I have a
pocketful of change.'

*

Kimura was a cheerful philistine. He took no interest in the
more refined aspects of Japanese culture, and had only the
vaguest notions about the various forms of Buddhism.
Nevertheless, he had seen a good many temples in his time,
and had been expecting Anraku-in to look much like the
famous ones in the historic cities of Kyoto, Nara and
Kamakura.

With vague images of spacious wooden buildings,
exquisite gardens and cools rooms floored with time-worn
tatami matting in mind, he had visualised the summer
school in a setting of calm austerity. He was therefore taken

34

aback by the appearance of the 'temple' when he stepped down from the bus and courteously assisted the lady from England to follow; but not so jolted that he failed to register and appreciate the fact that the underside of her forearm felt cool and satin-smooth.

The bus stop was immediately outside the entrance to a complex of modern buildings inside a handsome wall. The one which was immediately visible through the gateway and was evidently the most important might as far as Kimura was concerned have been a fair-sized hotel. The massive wooden signboard above its entrance bore, deeply incised and gilded, the three Chinese characters reading '*Anraku-in*', and for the first time since hearing the name, Kimura gave some thought to their meaning. '*Anraku*' unambiguously signified comfort or ease. The suffix '*-in*', however, could suggest not only a temple or retreat but alternatively an institution or college of some kind, as this clearly was.

'From the name I thought we were coming to a Buddhist temple,' he said. 'What *is* this place exactly?'

'It is a temple of some kind, but hardly Buddhist. It belongs to a curious sect.' Dr Kilpeck paused, and scrupulously corrected herself. 'I'm sorry, it's scarcely for me to judge. One of the so-called new religions, anyway, founded by a woman early in this century. I was given a pamphlet about it. I'm bound to say I don't begin to understand its theological principles, but so far as I can gather it's a little like Christian Science without the Christianity. They go in for faith-healing and so forth. You'd better ask Professor Kido about it. Shall we go inside?'

Heavy glass doors slid open automatically as they approached them, and they entered. Kimura shuddered involuntarily. 'One thing they certainly believe in is air conditioning, wouldn't you agree?'

Dr Kilpeck smiled. 'I should have warned you. One adjusts to it after a few minutes. This way.' To the left of the entrance was a reception desk with a telephone on it but it was unattended. The Englishwoman led the way through an ornate wooden door at the back of the lobby, which was spacious but unfurnished save for two easy chairs upholstered in shiny black plastic, and a low table on which had been placed a huge avant-garde 'flower' arrangement in a roughly rectangular ceramic trough. The arrangement was contrived in fact from a gnarled chunk of weathered wood, a number of oddly shaped stones embedded in an expanse of silver sand, and curved strips of sheet metal; and it rather appealed to Kimura.

On the other side of the door was a corridor about ten yards long, but Dr Kilpeck took only a few steps before pausing outside a plain, purely functional door. Its permanent white plastic sign identified the room behind it in Japanese as the 'General Affairs Section', but this was partially obscured by a temporary, lopsided one in English, written in spidery letters on a square of cardboard held in place by sticky tape. Whoever had prepared it had underestimated the amount of space required, and each word began in upper and ended in lower case, thus:

SUMMer
SCHOol
OFFIce

After scrutinising the home-made sign Kimura caught Dr Kilpeck's eye and grinned. 'I know,' she said. 'But it seems that Professor Kido did it himself and nobody wants to make him lose face by making a better-looking one.' She looked at her wrist-watch. 'Look, I think you'd better introduce yourself to Miss Yasuda. She speaks English, but it would obviously make more sense for you to talk to her in Japanese. And in any case, I don't want to miss another lecture. It's been a pleasure to meet you. Goodbye.'

She slid past him and disappeared into the lobby again so

quickly that Kimura had no time to respond, and stood for a second or two with his mouth still open before pulling himself together and tapping on the office door. There was no response, and after trying again he opened it a few inches and peeped in. There was nobody in the sizeable room, so he withdrew his head and closed the door again.

It was a pity that the interesting Philippa Kilpeck had taken herself off so abruptly, but Kimura had every hope of tracking her down again and pursuing her acquaintance before the day was out. In the meantime he was quite ready to charm Miss Yasuda instead, so he waited for a while in the corridor, hat in hand. However, there was still no sign of her after two minutes by the clock on the wall, and Kimura was by nature impatient. He therefore moved on along the corridor, past an elevator and a pair of much larger double doors which he tried but found to be locked. At the end of the corridor, a little further along, was a steel door with an illuminated green emergency exit sign over it.

The presence of the sign was to Kimura no guarantee that the door was unlocked, and he was pleasantly surprised to be able to open it and sniff at the rich warmth of the August sunshine outside. He slipped out, closing the door quietly behind him, and took in the scene.

He was standing at the top of a flight of four concrete steps leading down to a dusty little open space. Immediately opposite him was another building, in nondescript western style, smaller and altogether less imposing than the one from which he had just emerged. Perhaps because there were bicycle racks on either side of its entrance and it looked decidedly shabby and uncared-for, it reminded Kimura of a school and he decided that it must be a teaching block of some kind. He was struck by the absence of people, and puzzled because he had a distinct, rather eerie feeling that he was not alone. Then he thought he heard noises suggestive of shuffling feet coming from the right-hand side of the building he was facing. These were followed by the sound of a human voice, and Kimura went to investigate.

As soon as he could see round the corner Kimura realised that there was no mystery: it was simply that he had arrived in the middle of fire drill. There was a much bigger open space round there, on the far side of which were two more buildings. These were new-looking, and set in a Japanese-style garden. A motley assembly of about three dozen men and women were gathered in the open space with their backs to Kimura and facing a rotund little man who was addressing them with what seemed to be great earnestness. Given the season, he was dressed soberly enough, in dark trousers and a long-sleeved white shirt with a tie.

Kimura knew at once that he must be the person responsible for fire precautions, because he wore a red arm-band and on his head was the symbol of his status, a crumpled, peaked forage cap of khaki cloth. On the ground at his side was a fire extinguisher, and all at once he pointed at it dramatically, then seized the nozzle with one hand and depressed the plunger with the other. It was difficult from where Kimura was standing to see what, if anything, he was aiming at, but in fact the jet of liquid shot almost directly upwards into the air, much of it then descending to drench the demonstrator's own shirt and trouser legs.

It was the sort of thing that could happen to anybody, and Kimura felt quite sorry for the man, who managed eventually to direct the stream away from himself, struggling bravely with the nozzle until the extinguisher was empty. He then turned back to his audience and resumed his harangue.

Kimura was too far away to hear what he said, but evidently the drill and demonstration were being brought to a conclusion, whether prematurely or not he could not tell. At all events, before long the official was alone with his treacherous piece of equipment, a sodden, forlorn little figure watching while the witnesses to his discomfiture dispersed. A few of them made for bungalow-like buildings on the far side, but the majority started to head towards Kimura. He couldn't see Philippa Kilpeck in either group, but assumed that the secretary Miss Yasuda would now be returning to her post. There was no reason for Kimura to behave furtively, but he nevertheless retreated to the concrete steps leading to the main building, where he thought he would be able to intercept her.

Two foreigners were the first to round the corner. One was a stringy, fiftyish, deeply suntanned woman who was talking loudly. She had an unmistakably Australian accent. 'Serves him right, the pompous little twit. Honest, Manfred, I nearly died laughing even before he gave himself the old squirteroo treatment. He looked for all the world like something out of *The Bridge on the River Kwai* in that stupid hat.' She glanced briefly at Kimura but took no further notice of him, turning to the man beside her as if for his endorsement of her opinion. 'Don't tell me you haven't seen that movie?'

The man she called Manfred was of medium height and balding, though Kimura guessed he was probably not much over thirty. Seen on his own he would probably have looked ordinary enough, but with the Australian woman by his side he seemed to have an unnatural pallor. Kimura was a keen student of fashions in menswear and could see at a glance that his pale green short-sleeved shirt and fawn slacks had cost a lot of money. Yet they looked wrong on him. Manfred, he decided, was a person who ought to be discreetly suited at all times.

'I think not,' he said. 'The popular film as such is of small interest for me. But you know, it is sensible to become thoroughly familiar with the procedures to be observed in case of fire.' His manner was censorious, and the combination of the name Manfred and his way of pronouncing the 'th' sound made Kimura sure he was German. He and the woman went into the building that looked like a school as a young Japanese woman hurried round the corner, followed by a mixed group of Japanese and westerners. Kimura would have liked to linger and form an impression of the newcomers, but the young woman was upon him, one foot already on the concrete steps while those behind her went in after the German and the Australian woman.

'Excuse me, I'm sorry to trouble you. I was looking for the summer school secretary, but there's nobody in the office.'

'I am the secretary. I apologise for keeping you waiting. Please come inside.'

Kimura followed her up the steps and back inside the headquarters building, removing his hat as he did so and thinking again that it was like walking into a cold store. The chilly atmosphere seemed to suit the secretary, however. By the time they were both inside the office she was looking less flustered than she had outside, and turned to face him with a shy smile.

'I apologise once more. Good morning. I am Shoko Yasuda. How may I help you?'

Kimura bowed, took the smart leather case in which he kept his selection of name-cards from his little bag and extracted one that described him as a journalist. This he presented to Miss Yasuda with a flourish while introducing himself, after checking that he had another to give to the Director if and when he met him. Having once posed as a census official and then by mistake handed over a card on which he was described as a sales representative for the Encyclopaedia Britannica he was determined never to be caught out so embarrassingly again.

'I'm planning a series of features for the cultural page of the *Kobe Shimbun*,' he said, gazing tenderly into Miss Yasuda's eyes. 'Basically, on what we Japanese are doing to improve our image in the eyes of people in the west. I mean, to stop them thinking of us as just ruthless businessmen.'

Miss Yasuda took another look at the card in her hand. 'How interesting,' she said.

'Well, I hope they will be. Of course, to do much good they ought to be read by foreigners, not Japanese, but you never know, they might be picked up by the English-language papers too. Anyway, I dropped in at the Japan Foundation office in Kyoto to ask them about courses for foreigners in Japan and heard about this summer school in our own prefecture . . .' He paused and waited for some response. It had been galling to learn of the summer school from Otani, and on returning to his office Kimura had ticked off his assistant for failing to brief him in advance, and demanded full details. The faithful Migishima had drawn a blank with the prefectural tourist office but eventually obtained them from the Japan Foundation.

'I see.'

Having done so well with Philippa Kilpeck, Kimura was finding Miss Yasuda rather heavy going, and decided to take the bull by the horns. 'So what I'd like to do is to interview the director in private if he could spare me a few minutes, and then meet some of the foreigners taking part and find out how they're reacting to the course. I can speak English,' he added modestly.

Greatly to his surprise, Miss Yasuda's hand flew to her mouth in apparent horror, and beads of perspiration appeared on the bridge of her nose. It was some time before she seemed to regain control of her expression. 'Please wait a moment,' she said eventually in a timid little voice. 'Please take a seat.' Then she scuttled out of the door.

Five

Zenji Ono sat in the back of the luxurious car beside Keizo Hosoda, wishing he were somewhere, anywhere, else. The *yakuza* barons Takeuchi and Ikeda had decided that Hosoda was now not only redundant but a potential inconvenience, and that Ono had earned confirmation as his successor. In the nature of things it therefore fell to Ono to supervise this distasteful task personally, and he fully accepted the responsibility. Even so, he seriously doubted whether he had either the nerve or the acting ability to carry off his part in the proceedings successfully.

It was slightly reassuring to note that his unease seemed not to have communicated itself to Hosoda. That was not entirely surprising, perhaps. As boys they had been for a year or two inseparable friends, but their long association in adult life had never led to a revival of the old intimacy.

Hosoda the man had always been too unpredictable for Ono the man to approach emotionally. From time to time Ono had discerned more than a hint of sentimentality underlying the practised charm; most recently at the celebration lunch in Nara when Hosoda in the course of his maudlin speech had remembered his birthday. On such occasions in the past it had occasionally occurred to Ono that Hosoda might actually *like* him. Invariably, however, that impression had soon been dispelled by one of Hosoda's frightening outbursts of anger, or by some arrogantly high-handed behaviour on his part, so Ono kept his distance even when Hosoda seemed to be in the mood to regard him as a crony. Then again, while Hosoda was in jail it had been necessary for their dealings to be particularly circumspect, and five years was a long time.

All in all, therefore, it was unlikely that Hosoda would have retained any clear impression of what Ono's normal manner towards him had been before his imprisonment, or notice anything odd about it now. So perhaps he was worrying unnecessarily, especially as there wasn't much that Hosoda could do about it even if he did smell a rat. The big car with the smoked glass rear windows belonged to Takeuchi, as did the loyalties of the neatly uniformed, white-gloved man driving it. Ono knew that there was a gun in the glove compartment, and that it would be used without hesitation when the time came. It wasn't as if he was expected to wield it himself – and in any case for the present all he had to do was sit there and chat to Hosoda.

They were bound for the northern outskirts of Kobe and the site of an Elite Property Developments project now nearing completion. The Royal Park Heights estate was the company's most ambitious venture to date, and Hosoda was boyishly excited at the prospect of seeing it at last. The majority of the luxury apartments in the five blocks under construction at the huge site carved out of the hillside were already sold, and Ono was confident that the remainder would be taken well before they were ready for occupation. Actual and potential purchasers were enthused by the thought of living in one of the state-of-the-art, earthquake- and typhoon-proof buildings that had generated a lot of interest, and not only in specialist architectural journals.

The glossy brochure put out by Elite Property Developments described the technical achievements of those responsible for the design and construction of these so-called 'smart' buildings, but reasonably enough stressed the delights in store for those who would live on the estate. First came the peace of mind arising from total security: magic eye video cameras and answerphone devices for the identification of callers were to be linked not only to the front doors of individual apartments but also to their separate garages and to a twenty-four hour security office at the massive main gates.

Then, each apartment was of course to be fully wired for both cable and broadcast television, and would come equipped with telephones and a fax machine. That was only to be expected; but even in Japan it was still going to be something of a novelty for householders to be able to ring up their homes from wherever they happened to be and instruct an ever-attentive electronic control system to adjust the central heating or airconditioning, record a favourite television or radio programme on tape, mix, knead and bake a loaf of bread or cook the dinner.

Almost as an afterthought the promotional material pointed out that the Royal Park Heights estate was ideally situated within easy walking distance of New Kobe Station. There one could step directly on to what foreigners insisted on calling a bullet train and be in Osaka in twenty minutes or so, or Tokyo in about three and a half hours; or one could take the subway and arrive in downtown Kobe in a few minutes. Royal Park Heights seemed certain to become *the* address for sophisticated folk in the Kansai area of western Japan, and it was going to be hard to upstage people who had it printed on their name-cards.

Ono had planned the precise timing of their visit with care, on the basis of the most recent weekly progress report and detailed flow charts submitted to his office by the site manager. As president of Elite Property Developments he had already carried out two or three formal inspections of the site while the apartment blocks were going up. On those occasions he had been escorted by a phalanx of deferential architects, quantity surveyors and other specialists, and had posed for photographs wearing a hard hat – a special white one that stood out like a lily in a clump of daffodils.

This time the site manager had not been warned of an

impending visit by the exalted Mr Ono. Nor was the manager or anyone else of consequence who knew him by sight
likely to notice his arrival. All the supervisory staff were
scheduled to be in conference between two and three, and it
was now just ten past two. The car swept on to the site,
attracting no more than a sour but cursory glance from the
checker at the gate. His job was to book in truck-loads of
building materials, not to concern himself with rich people
who rolled up in flashy cars to be shown round the display
flat by one of the sales staff he despised – nothing to choose
between the smarmy men and the toffee-nosed glamour
girls with their cutesy-pie voices in his opinion.

'Round to the right here,' Ono said to the driver. 'Behind
that block where they're working on the porch.' He turned
to Hosoda, who had lowered the electrically operated
window on his side and was gazing out with an air of lively
interest. 'The only basic construction job still to be done is
on the restaurant, and that won't take long now. You may
remember, almost the last time I came to see you I mentioned we'd been having a bit of trouble with the planning
authority over one corner of the site. Seems there was some
sort of temple here hundreds of years ago, but we persuaded
the appropriate official to give the go-ahead in the end. I'll
show you that area first, and then we'll have a look at the
apartment I've reserved for you.'

A minute or two later the driver stopped the car behind
the block Ono had indicated, and jumped out to open the
rear door on Hosoda's side. Ono slid across and followed
Hosoda out. 'I'll lead the way, shall I?' he enquired solici-
tously. 'I think we can be excused for not wearing hard hats
round the back here. As you can see, there are no workmen
about on this side. It'll be swarming when they put in the
foundations of the restaurant annex.'

There was, in fact, just one man in view, apart from their
chauffeur who was now following a few yards behind as
Ono and Hosoda wandered along. That was the operator of

a power shovel, who was tidying the sides of a fair-sized, straight-sided hole some two metres deep. Hosoda walked over to it.

'Amazing how these fellows can handle those massive things so delicately. Little touches here and there, for all the world like a surgeon taking somebody's appendix out.' He looked across at the operator and gave him a thumbs-up sign.

'Nice of you to encourage him,' Ono said. 'Good management practice, that.'

He had never expected Hosoda to be so cooperative. The single bullet fired into the back of his head by the chauffeur toppled the big man straight into the hole. The power shovel operator really was an expert. He contrived to make the engine of his machine emit a crescendo of noise at the precise moment the shot was fired, completely disguising it; and within fewer than ten minutes had filled in and smoothed over the grave of Keizo Hosoda.

Ono managed to hold down the bile that kept rising up to his throat, and waved at the workman. '*Gokurosama deshita!* Well done!' he called to him in a voice that wavered too much for his liking. Then he turned to the chauffeur. '*Gokurosama deshita.* Now for heaven's sake let's get out of here.'

The big glossy limousine had to wait just inside the gates for a few minutes to allow a convoy of half a dozen ready-mix cement trucks to pass through, their huge containers growling and churning. They were on their way to discharge their loads into the excavations at the back of the block Ono had just left, and within an hour Hosoda's remains would be under not only two metres of earth, but a further twenty-five centimetres of wet concrete.

Six

When Kimura eventually found himself ensconced in the small office provided for the use of the academic director of the international summer school and face to face with Professor Minoru Kido, he remained at a loss to account for the previous curious behaviour of the secretary, Shoko Yasuda. For she had struck Kimura initially as being a composed sort of young woman, unlikely to go in fear and trembling of her boss; especially as it seemed probable that she was working for him only for the duration of the school.

Certainly, and leaving aside the fact that his shirt and trousers were obviously still damp and must be making him very uncomfortable as they dried in the frigid conditioned air inside the building, there was nothing much about Kido at close quarters that made him seem intimidating or impressive. He didn't cut quite such a ludicrous figure as he had in his silly hat while addressing the assembled students during fire drill and ineptly demonstrating the use of the extinguisher, but he did look gauche and ill coordinated.

Kido was, Kimura surmised, a man in his late forties or early fifties, and shaped somewhat like two pears, one perched on top of the other. He was bulky about the hips and bottom, but narrow in the shoulder, and the slenderness of his neck was emphasised by the fact that it rose, turtle-like, from a shirt collar a couple of sizes too big. The head it supported was also oddly shaped, in that Kido had a broad, almost aggressive-looking jawline, but his forehead was comparatively narrow, the few strands of hair arranged across his otherwise bald scalp doing nothing to disguise its meagre dimensions.

'It's extremely good of you to receive me without an appointment, *sensei*,' Kimura began after the ritual exchange of name-cards. It was quite in order, indeed necessary, to read such cards on receipt, in order to appraise the information they carried, for only then could each employ the appropriate level of polite language in addressing the other party. Like most other mature, sophisticated Japanese, Kimura had learned to do this in a couple of seconds at most, and was amused to note that Kido studied the card describing him as a freelance journalist for an unusually long time. When he did speak he was obviously still having trouble in deciding how to handle that unusual creature in Japan, a well-dressed, urbane person apparently devoid of rank or status in a recognised organisation.

'Yes, well, ah . . . Mr Kimura. In what way can I assist you?'

Kimura decided to help him out. He had learned from Kido's own card that he was a man of high professional standing: professor of archaeology at one of the wealthier and more prestigious private universities in the Kansai area, and also the current chairman of the Hyogo prefectural government's advisory committee on historical monuments. So no matter what he looked like, he rated kid-glove treatment.

'I do realise it's highly irregular for me to have approached such an eminent scholar in this way, sir. Normally I should of course have asked the features editor at the *Kobe Shimbun* to call or write to you in advance and explain the series I'm working on, then made a proper appointment through your secretary.'

Kido said nothing but nodded almost imperceptibly, making it clear that he agreed that this would indeed have been the right and proper thing to do.

'But the fact is that until an hour or so ago I had no idea

that this fascinating project was under way here at the Anraku-in,' Kimura lied with the easy fluency acquired through long practice. 'If I hadn't had the good fortune to get into conversation with one of your students quite by chance at the Sasayama bus terminal, I should probably never have found my way here. But once I had, it seemed too good a chance to miss, so I ventured to ask if you might possibly spare me a few minutes of your time. Needless to say, I'll quite understand if you'd prefer me to come back another day.'

Kimura mentally crossed his fingers. He had a friend on the editorial staff of the *Kobe Shimbun* who could if necessary be persuaded to support his spur-of-the-moment story, but it seemed reasonable to hope that having been disturbed anyway, Kido would prefer to deal with him on the spot and then be rid of him.

'That won't be necessary. We welcome publicity of the right kind for our summer school, so by all means ask me whatever general questions you wish. You say you heard about our project from one of the students? Who was that, may I ask?'

'A British lady. Dr Philippa Kilpeck. She was most helpful and informative.'

A smile of obvious warmth and sincerity illuminated Professor Kido's face for a moment before he swung round abruptly in his chair, snatched a handkerchief from his trouser pocket and sneezed violently into it.

'I do apologise,' he then said huskily, his back still turned to Kimura. Kimura for his part courteously affected not to notice the breach of etiquette constituted by a public sneeze and nose-blowing. The poor fellow was very likely landing himself with a severe chill as a consequence of not changing his clothes after the fiasco with the fire extinguisher.

'Yes. Dr Kilpeck is a fine scholar and a delightful person,' Kido said when he had eventually recovered from the sneeze and turned to face Kimura again. 'But she does not speak Japanese, so how – of course, I was forgetting. The secretary mentioned that you told her you can speak English.' Kido was not looking at all well, and after failing to suppress a shudder, obviously came to a decision. 'Mr Kimura, I think I must after all ask you to excuse me. I am not quite myself at the moment, but perhaps you would like to speak instead to my American co-director. Mr Ashley is a kind of official of the organisation that owns the Anraku-in, and in any case responsible for the international dimension to this school. I'm sure he will be pleased to introduce you to some of the foreign participants.'

*

'Sure,' Bill Ashley said. 'Right after lunch they go into free activity time until three thirty.' He grinned. 'For one or two of the older folk free activity tends to take the form of a nap, but there'll be plenty of people around who'll be glad to talk with you.'

In spite of the fact that he was of the male sex and had to be pushing sixty, Ashley was Kimura's kind of foreigner. By the time he introduced them to each other, Kido had been looking distinctly seedy, and he left them almost at once and headed for the range of single-storey buildings that, Ashley explained, contained living quarters for the summer school staff and the overseas participants. There wasn't room for everybody, but most of the Japanese students taking part were from the Kansai area. These were encouraged to attend on a daily basis and to go home each evening, while those from further afield made their own arrangements to stay at inns in the district.

Left to themselves, the two men hit it off at once, Ashley proving to be a chatty and amusing companion as they strolled in a leisurely way round the compound in which the fire drill had been staged. Until Kido left them the American had spoken Japanese very well, but then switched to English and cheerfully suggested after a minute or two that they should stick to that, since Kimura was, as he put it, clearly a major league linguist while he himself just managed to get by in Japanese.

Within twenty minutes or so Kimura had learned that Ashley, whose name he now thought was vaguely familiar to him, had lived in Japan since the early nineteen-fifties, having first arrived as a GI towards the end of the Occupation. Deciding to stay on after getting out of the US Army he'd gone first into the travel business, working as a courier showing groups of American tourists the sights of Nikko, Kamakura, Kyoto and Nara; and then set himself up as a dealer in old maps, wood-block prints and what he irreverently called nineteenth-century junk.

'You bet, I turned my hand to all manner of things over the years. Owned an American-style bar for a while in Yokohama, did agency work for some two-bit American companies looking for business here, you name it. But I kept coming back to what I like best, which is messing around the edges of Japanese culture and making a reasonably honest buck out of it. So when the outfit that runs Anraku-in were looking for an American to handle their English language PR operation and made me an offer, I said okay, why not? That was around eighteen months ago.'

'So is this the first international summer school to be held here?'

'I guess you could say so. Quite a few of what you Japanese call "new religions" are pretty strong on cultural activities, as I'm sure you know. I guess a guy like you also knows that the associated activity often stands up a whole lot better than the religion, with some pretty weird ideas being promoted alongside high cultural standards. I don't mind telling you my employers are typical. A good many gaijin culture-vultures have found their way here individually over the years, but this is the first time we've offered a properly organised residential course.'

'Off the record, Mr Ashley, would I be right to assume from what you say that you're not exactly a true believer?'

Ashley stopped, and fixed Kimura with a disconcertingly penetrating stare from a pair of keen grey eyes. '*Strictly* off the record, Mr Kimura, no, I'm not. In fact, I'd like you to regard our conversation up to this point as personal and private; and to start on the interview now, on the understanding that it's going to be about the summer school, and not at all about William J. Ashley. Except as spokesman and administrative co-director, right?'

'Right.'

'Good. Then I can inform you that this first International Summer School on the Traditional Arts and Crafts of Japan, though taking place here at the Anraku-in, is in no sense a religious project. Few if any of the participating students have any connection with the organisation that owns the premises, nor do any of the teaching staff, all of whom are distinguished experts in their respective fields.'

Kimura nodded. 'Understood. Would you care to tell me a little about the subjects of study, and the teaching staff?'

'Surely. Many of the subjects covered are dealt with purely descriptively, in the course of lectures on relevant aspects of Japanese history. It isn't feasible to offer live demonstrations, much less practical instruction in, well, *kemari* for example – that's a kind of football that used to be played by the Emperor's courtiers many centuries ago. Or horseback archery. Though even in those two specific cases students can see videos of these activities. Another example. The academic director, Professor Kido, is a very well-known archaeologist and currently involved in one or two digs. Students have an opportunity to visit the sites concerned, but are obviously interested in what the discoveries made there are telling us about Japanese culture, not the actual digging. And so on and so forth.'

'But there are some things the students can actually try their hands at, are there?'

'Yes, indeed, a wide range. There's a fully equipped pottery workshop, supervised by a master potter from Hagi. Students can learn how to make Japanese paper, and have lessons in calligraphy. They can make Japanese kites, weave baskets, study flower arrangement, take part in an authentic tea ceremony, and so on.'

'All at a pretty basic level, though, I imagine?'

'Not necessarily. Some of the so-called students are themselves experts. I guess the most distinguished is a French Japanologist, Professor Leclerc. He's an archaeologist too, an old friend and long-time associate of Kido. He's been in and out of Japan dozens of times over the past twenty-five years and more and certainly has nothing to learn from us. Then there's a German here, name of Manfred Weisse, who's a very well-known teacher of Chinese and Japanese calligraphy in the west. Howard Bayliss is an attorney from Boston who's reckoned to be the top amateur expert on samurai armour outside Japan. And a British historian—'

'Dr Kilpeck. Yes, I've met her.'

'Have you, now.'

'Only briefly. What's she particularly interested in?'

'I'm not sure. Something to do with interpreting old documents. We'll probably find her working in the library after lunch, and you can ask her yourself.'

Ashley glanced at his watch and winked at Kimura. 'And it's lunchtime right now, so let's go eat, and slip off the record again for a while, shall we? I've bored myself to death with all that public relations stuff. So you've met our Philippa, have you? What did you think of her?'

'Impressive.'

'You can say that again – oh, hi there, Maggie. Hungry? Come on over, I want you to meet Jiro Kimura. He's a reporter, about to tell the world what a great crowd we have here. Mr Kimura, this is Maggie Threlfall, from Awstrylia. That is how you pronounce it, Maggie?'

'Hopeless, hopeless, you ignorant Yank. You want lessons in Strine, you can pay for 'em. G'day to you, Kimura-san.' It was the woman Kimura had seen earlier, talking to the calligrapher Manfred Weisse. She now seized his hand and pumped it vigorously. 'Come to expose this old fraud, have you?' She punched the grinning Ashley on the upper arm. They obviously liked each other a lot, and Kimura envied them their lack of inhibition. It was hard to imagine two Japanese of their generation behaving in that way to each other even in private; inconceivable that they could do so in public.

'Maggie teaches Japanese in Adelaide, believe it or not. Came here with the idea of getting a lesson or two ahead of her students, I reckon.'

'You mean you offer Japanese language instruction too?'

'We sure do, but that's enough shop for now. Here come Howard and Inger. Come on, I'll introduce you and buy you all a beer.'

*

About two hours later Kimura was beginning to think he had absorbed enough for one day, especially as nothing he had heard or seen, apart from the odd reaction of the secretary Shoko Yasuda when he had asked to meet the director, suggested that anything might be amiss about the summer school. He had seen Michiko Yanagida at a distance in the dining hall, holding forth to an attentive circle of students, but had no fear that she would recognise him, for they had never in fact met. He would have liked to ask her to enlarge on the fears she had expressed to her brother-in-law, but that was out of the question while he was sailing under false colours.

He had duly met Howard Bayliss the lawyer and authority on samurai armour, and Inger Lindblad, an opulent-looking, middle-aged Danish woman. During their conversation Ms Lindblad spotted and hailed the eminent French scholar Professor Maximilian Leclerc, who was sauntering across the open space as elegantly as if he were taking the air in the Tuileries Gardens in Paris. Leclerc merely raised his silver-topped stick in casual salute and continued. Kimura had long been cultivating a boulevardier image for himself and hoped he would look as stylish at Leclerc's age.

After parting from the Danish woman Kimura had visited and dutifully photographed the studio in which three Japanese and a young Belgian couple were making paper under the direction of a kindly-looking Japanese expert called Miyamoto, and been shown some impressive examples of Manfred Weisse's calligraphy. He and Bill Ashley were on their way to the library in the imposing main building when Kimura noticed the secretary Shoko Yasuda emerge from the living quarters, pause and look around in an agitated way. Then, seeing Ashley, she ran towards them.

'Miss Yasuda seems to want you in a hurry,' Kimura said, and politely moved away to allow her to speak to Ashley privately. In fact he remained near enough to see that she was in obvious distress, and clearly urging Ashley to go with her to the living quarters. Twenty years of police training and experience yelled at him to follow, but Kimura managed to stay where he was and play the interested visitor, taking a few more photographs of the buildings, particularly when he could include a couple of students in the picture.

'You're still here, then, Mr Kimura.'

He wheeled round to discover Philippa Kilpeck at his elbow. 'Indeed I am. And very much indebted to you for telling me about this place. Ah, as a matter of fact Mr Ashley was about to take me over to the library to see if we could find you, but he had some urgent business to attend to over in the residential block, so I was just—' He broke off, cocking his ear at the unmistakeable two tone sound of a siren, growing rapidly louder. 'Sorry, that's an ambulance,' he explained. 'Seems to be heading in this direction.'

Within a couple of minutes Kimura had no further need to think of excuses for hastening over to the residential buildings to find out why Miss Yasuda had summoned Ashley so urgently. The arrival of the ambulance outside them immediately attracted a group of curious onlookers, and when a couple of minutes later one of the ambulance men emerged to fetch a stretcher he was followed by two or three other people from inside the building who soon spread the word that the patient was Professor Kido.

Then, when they carried him out, the murmur of conversation was succeeded by a stunned silence, for a blanket covered the face of the figure on the stretcher, and the bearers were obviously no longer in a hurry.

In spite of the dramatic turn of events, Kimura was disposed to maintain his cover at least for the time being, and would probably have done so, had not Maggie Threlfall's voice been the first to break the silence.

'Well, they got the poor old bugger this time. Third time lucky for somebody.'

Seven

The commander of the Hyogo prefectural police force reached for his personal seal. A stubby rod of ivory, cylindrical in section and about two inches long and half an inch in diameter, it nestled in a velvet-lined compartment in the neat little hinged, leather-covered case that usually lay open on his desk during office hours. Carved in relief on its business end were the two Chinese characters reading 'Otani', within a circle, while the other end had been exquisitely fashioned into a Chinese lion with its left forepaw balanced on a sphere. Tiny as it was, the carving was full of life and humour, and Otani was fond of his seal. Hanae had found it in an antique shop many years before and given it to him, after having the name it had originally borne removed and his own put in its place. It would cost a fortune to have such a thing made to order, even if one could find a craftsman capable of doing the work.

Touching the end to the little red inkpad incorporated into its case, Otani sealed the last two of the reports he had read and approved that morning, sat back and stretched. It was getting on for twelve noon and he was tired of paperwork. These days he rarely asked Hanae to make him a *bento* to eat in the office, and the lovely old lacquer lunchbox that had belonged to his father lay untouched on a kitchen shelf for weeks on end. Hanae's bento were invariably delicious and never failed to include 'something from the sea and something from the mountains', but with a choice of literally hundreds of places to eat lunch in Kobe within ten minutes walk from police headquarters, it seemed hardly fair to go on putting her to the trouble of preparing one for him.

So many of the old habits and pleasures, formerly taken for granted, seemed to be dying out. There was no time for grace and the leisurely appreciation of good things in the helter-skelter world of the new Japan, with its twenty-four-hour convenience stores, wall-to-wall muzak and strident advertising. In Japanese inns they played tape-recordings of bird-song in the mornings because there were no living song-birds left anywhere near human habitations. Even a good many *sushi* bars were automated, with customers helping themselves from the plates of sushi passing before them on an endless belt, and topping up their beakers of green tea from the dispensers mounted at intervals along the counter. There were still places where one was made to feel welcome, and could have a chat with the master while he put together a proper, old-fashioned feast, but they were expensive and getting a lot harder to find.

Otani sighed, shook his head sadly and reached over to switch off the big electric fan beside his desk. Then he made his way out of his office and along the corridor. At least the strip of coconut matting had been there as long as he had himself, and the photographs of all his predecessors. How horrified they would have been, even the most recent, if anyone had predicted that a day would come when a superintendent of police would allow himself to be seen in his shirtsleeves by his subordinates, much less go out to lunch thus improperly dressed!

The thought put Otani into a somewhat better humour, and when, while still going down the main staircase, he saw Inspector Hara crossing the lobby, he waylaid him.

'Inspector! Have you a moment?'

'Of course, sir.' Hara stood where he was, all courteous attention, until Otani joined him.

'I mustn't detain you if you're rushing off somewhere.'

'I am always at your disposal, sir.'

Otani suppressed the temptation to tease him. Kimura often positively begged to have his leg pulled and invariably bounced back as bumptious as ever within five minutes, but Hara was altogether less easy to read.

'Actually, I'm on my way to find some lunch myself.' A revolutionary idea popped into Otani's mind. 'Have you had yours yet?'

'No, sir. I was intending to go out after returning these papers to my office.'

'I wonder, would you by any chance care to join me? Please don't hesitate to say if you have other plans.'

'I should be delighted, but . . .' Hara rather dubiously eyed the papers he was carrying.

'Good. Get rid of your papers by all means. I'll wait for you here.'

Fifteen minutes later they were seated at a comparatively quiet corner table in an Italian-style restaurant which, because it was more up-market than the sort frequented by most 'salarymen' and 'office ladies' at lunchtime, was also markedly less busy. Having made it clear, over Hara's protests, that the meal was on him, Otani chose the most expensive of the three set lunches, the so-called 'A-Course'. This consisted of minestrone followed by veal marsala with spaghetti and the inevitable *puriin* or caramel custard to follow. A glass of red wine was included in the price, and Otani gazed over the top of his at Hara.

'I should have suggested this months ago,' he said. 'I'm sorry. As you know, I often go off with Ninja to one of his horrible snack bar places for curry-rice or Chinese noodles, and occasionally somewhere a bit more sophisticated with Kimura.'

'Yes, but you've known them a lot longer than me,' Hara said equably. Otani noticed with interest that so long as they had been talking shop while walking to the restaurant, his companion had remained in character as the deferential subordinate. Now, however, he had stopped calling him sir and was apparently quite relaxed.

'It's understandable that you should want to take your time over sizing me up. I've very much appreciated the way you've brought me into your inner cabinet.'

'Ah.' Otani lowered his head in momentary confusion and slurped up a spoonful of minestrone. 'Unlike your predecessor, you mean. Yes, well, I could hardly expect you not to have found out all about Sakamoto, poor fellow. The fact of the matter is that I never could stand him, and neither could Ninja or Kimura. It's hard to confide in a man apparently devoid of human feelings. How wrong we all were! Believe me, I've had many a bad night telling myself that if only I'd made an effort to treat him better he might not have been driven to do what he did.'

Hara's pale moon face was illuminated by a distinctly cheeky grin. 'So you've invited me out to lunch to make sure you won't have to cope with another crazy head of CID one of these days.' Then, just as Otani was beginning to think that informality could be taken too far a lot too fast, Hara pulled himself up. 'I'm sorry, sir, that remark was in very poor taste.' Otani made a dismissive gesture, but Hara went on. 'I do realise that the Sakamoto affair must have been extraordinarily painful for you. I must admit that for the first few months after I was transferred here I was convinced you couldn't stand me either. That you thought I was a pompous know-all.'

Otani smiled faintly. 'It did take me a while to see through that schoolmaster style of yours,' he admitted. 'But there had to be some good reason why Ninja Noguchi took to you from the start. And when Kimura started to get on terms with you too, well, I belatedly realised I was all wrong. Ninja told me he'd been to your flat, and that you were quite different at home. So why do you put on that act in the office? If you don't mind my asking.'

'In the office, you scare me.'

'*What?*'

'Yes. You make me feel totally inadequate. Superintendent, I don't think you can have the slightest idea what it's like to be assigned to be responsible for CID work under the most famous and successful police detective in Japan. And to watch your technique at close quarters. Is it so surprising that I weigh every word I say to you in that office?'

'Come now, Hara, you're talking nonsense. These days I'm just an administrator trying to squeeze money out of the prefectural government and a PR man handing out prizes to Road Safety Week organisers.'

'Forgive me if I beg to differ,' Hara said. 'It was you who spotted Hosoda's name outside the Nara Hotel and managed to turn it into a complete list of associates of his important enough to be present at his welcome-out-of-jail party.'

'That was pure luck. Anyway, how are you and Ninja getting on with your analysis of that invitation list?'

'Not too badly. Ninja already knew a lot about the two yakuza bosses, needless to say. Takeuchi and Ikeda. And between us we've managed to place most of the others where they belong in the hierarchy. The odd man out among the names you jotted down is Zenji Ono. You don't happen to remember where he was supposed to sit, do you?'

Otani pulled a face and shook his head. 'There you are, no further need to be impressed, Hara. A proper detective would have drawn a plan of that table layout. I don't even recall writing down the name, much less where his card was. What's odd about him, anyway?'

'Well, in the first place there's no record of a crook with that name. There is a pretty big wheel in the district called Zenji Ono, but so far as we know he's legitimate. Trained as a lawyer, now president of a property development company.'

Otani thought about it and then shrugged. 'I'm not saying every single one's a crook, but scratch a property developer and you might well find a yakuza, or friend of one. Maybe he's just good at covering his tracks. As Hosoda himself seems to have been, if your greenmailing idea holds up. I presume you're having your people find out more about this Ono?'

'Of course, and Ninja has his ear to the ground too. The more immediate problem concerns the guest of honour.'

'Hosoda himself?'

'That's right. He seems to have disappeared.'

'Oh, come on. He's only been out a few days. Entitled to go away for a holiday, wouldn't you think?'

'No doubt, but Ninja has been picking up whispers here and there. To the effect that somebody might possibly have put out a contract on him.'

'Really? Well, that would be an interesting development indeed. Not the actor fellow he shot in Osaka, surely?'

'I did say it's only a whisper. We can hardly go worrying our heads about the welfare of the Hosodas of this world on that sort of basis.'

Otani picked up the bill and glanced into Hara's coffee cup. 'Finished? Good, we'd better be getting along.' Having paid at the cash desk by the door, he followed Hara out of the restaurant and they rode the escalator up from the bowels of the Sannomiya underground mall to ground level. There Hara showed some signs of reverting to his stiff official manner, and Otani brushed off his effusive expressions of gratitude for the meal.

'Not at all, not at all, we must do it again some time. You know, on the way here I was so busy picking your brains about this genetic fingerprinting technique that I quite forgot to ask if there's been any word from Kimura. Wasn't he supposed to be in the country today? The temple my sister-in-law's worried about?'

'Anraku-in. Yes, sir, that is correct. I had assumed that he would in any case report to you on his return.'

'Yes, I dare say he will, unless he gets distracted by some

glamorous foreign woman and forgets why he's there. Tell you what, Hara, you go on ahead if you don't mind. I'm sure you've got a million things waiting for you. I just want to pop into the Maruzen bookstore and have a bit of a browse. Thank you for your company, you've given me a lot to think about.'

Left to himself, Otani did saunter to the big bookstore and cast a casual eye over the crime fiction section. Among the current crop of new translations there was an Ed McBain he was tempted to buy, and a Tony Hillerman. He had a soft spot for Joe Leaphorn and Jim Chee, not to mention the boys in the 87th Precinct, but there was nothing quite like a vintage Nero Wolfe, he always claimed.

The Case of the Modest Detective, he murmured under his breath, thinking about Hara's embarrassing eulogy; and then *The Guest of Honour Regrets.* Ninja wouldn't have mentioned having picked up rumours about Keizo Hosoda to Hara unless he was inclined to give them some credence . . . oh well, if there was a mystery, the pair of them could sort it out between them. Meantime Kimura was no doubt enjoying himself among the foreigners; possibly even attempting to flirt with sister-in-law Michiko. Otani rather hoped he would ring in before the end of the afternoon. Hanae would be interested to hear what if anything he came up with.

Eight

Kimura's first thought was to rush to the summer school office and make use of the telephone there while Ashley and Miss Yasuda were otherwise occupied, but one is seldom very far from a payphone in Japan, and he wanted to avoid even the slightest risk of being overheard. So he took the opportunity provided by the general hubbub that followed Maggie Threlfall's laconic announcement to slip away, left the Anraku-in premises altogether and walked quickly towards a cluster of little shops about a hundred yards beyond the main gates. He found a payphone outside a *sake* shop, began to dial the emergency number 109–110 but then thought better of it and instead inserted one of the several prepaid phonecards he always had about him into the slot and punched out the direct line number for CID section at headquarters in Kobe. A calm female voice answered.

'Is that you, Junko-san? Kimura here, Foreign Affairs Section. Is Hara there? I see. Never mind. I need your help urgently, and I'm sure he'll give covering approval. I'm speaking from Sasayama north of Kobe. A temple of some sort called Anraku-in. Hara knows all about it – what's that? He's told you about the summer school? Excellent, that'll save me a lot of breath. Now listen. The academic director, Professor Minoru Kido, has died suddenly and been taken away in an ambulance. Cause of death not known. At present I'm passing myself off as a journalist and I think it would be best to stay under that cover for the time being. What I want you to do right away is check with the local ambulance station here and find out where they'll have taken Kido. Then talk to whoever you can get hold of in some sort of authority at Sasayama police station and tip him off in confidence. Two essential points. An autopsy must be carried out. They'd probably have done one in any case, but the pathologist must be told on the quiet to be ultra-careful. Second, the Sasayama police are to note carefully when and by whom at Anraku-in they're notified of the death, and in precisely what terms. Got all that? Good. Tell Hara I'll call him in an hour or two, before the end of the afternoon, anyway.'

Kimura replaced the receiver and retrieved his phonecard, which as it happened was one handed out as a form of advertising by a bar he occasionally patronised. It had a photograph of one of their best-looking hostesses on the back. Lucky it had been Woman Senior Detective Junko Migishima on the line. One of the brightest stars of the prefectural CID, Junko was married to one of Kimura's own staff and they had often worked together. He had no doubt whatever that within a very few minutes she would have done everything necessary, and that Hara would have been fully briefed by the time he did talk to him. Meantime, he had some sniffing around to do at Anraku-in.

On the way back Kimura looked at his watch, an elegant piece of wrist decoration which had unfortunately stopped, as his watches had a habit of doing. So he delved into his trouser pocket and took out a shocking pink plastic one with a picture of the Sesame Street puppet Kermit the Frog on the dial. It had been given to him at his local branch of the Dai-Ichi Kangyo Bank last time he had needed a new paying-in book, had probably cost the price of a cup of coffee, and, maddeningly, kept perfect time.

It was just after three-fifteen, and Kimura remembered Ashley mentioning that the students' free time was due to end at three-thirty – assuming that the summer school would carry on at all following the unexpected demise of its academic director. He was in some doubt as to what to do next. Clearly it was out of the question to attempt to talk to either Ashley or Miss Yasuda unless he were to abandon his cover story and announce his true identity.

Nor would it be appropriate at this stage to seek out Professor Michiko Yanagida and confide in her. She could hardly deny having expressed forebodings to her brother-in-law, and in doing so had unquestionably expected him to have the situation looked into. There were nevertheless good reasons why before doing that he should try in the guise of journalist to extract as much information as possible from other parties, notably the foreign participants. The obvious person to begin with was the outspoken Australian Maggie Threlfall. She was obviously a born gossip and it ought to be possible to get her to enlarge on her startling remark.

People were standing about in couples and small groups in the compound when Kimura arrived back there, but he couldn't see Maggie Threlfall among them. He did however spot Philippa Kilpeck, who detached herself from one of the groups and came over to meet him as he approached.

'I apologise for leaving you like that in all the excitement, Dr Kilpeck. Newspaperman's instincts made me go find a phone, I'm afraid. It'll probably only make a couple of paragraphs on an inside page, but they'll pay me for it. I expect you think that ghoulish and unfeeling.'

She shrugged. 'Nobody familiar with the practices of British reporters could be surprised. When you left I assumed you were on your way to do something you are paid to do.' She held Kimura's eye for a moment and then abruptly turned her head away.

Kimura tucked away the slightly mysterious form of words she had used to think about later, and tried to inject warmth and sympathy into his voice. 'You're upset, of course. Perhaps you'll allow me to say that I am, too. I never set eyes on Professor Kido before this morning, and I was in his company for no more than ten minutes or so altogether. But I can well believe he'll be much missed.'

'Yes. He will.'

'You met him yourself only recently, I guess?'

'No, last year. He came to England. Mainly to visit a few digs and meet archaeologists, of course, but he also spent some time at the Institute for Historical Research in London. Otherwise I should probably never have heard of this summer school. I certainly wouldn't be here, and now . . .'

'You liked him.'

'Very much. Although my own field is quite remote from his, he has been enormously helpful to me and put me in touch with Japanese historians I knew only by name, through their publications.'

'Dr Kilpeck, I couldn't help overhearing what the Australian lady said a while ago.'

Anger flared in her eyes. 'Of course you couldn't. She fully intended to be overheard.'

'And this morning, after the fire drill, she was talking pretty loudly about Professor Kido to the German calligrapher, Mr Weisse. Then she was kind of making fun of him, but this afternoon she seemed to be implying—'

'I know quite well what she was implying, Mr Kimura, and I think it most unfortunate that you were there. Professor Kido was a kind and sensitive man, and a scholar of the utmost integrity. But I suppose the newspapers will have no interest in reporting that kind of opinion. Unfounded insinuations and malicious speculation sell many more copies, I'm sure. Now if you will excuse me, I have other things to do.'

*

'I don't know why I bother standing here,' Otani said. 'You can't see a thing this time of the year. Too much moisture in the atmosphere.' He turned away from the glazed part of the window in the big upstairs room in the old house on the foothills of Mount Rokko east of Kobe, and watched Hanae fetching the futons from the cupboard and laying out their bedding directly on the floor. The golden tatami matting gleamed in the soft light from the small electric lamp, the only illumination in the room.

'Never mind,' Hanae said, busily stuffing their little hard pillows into clean slips. 'You know the Inland Sea's still there, even if you can't see it.'

'For the time being,' Otani said gloomily, and Hanae glanced up at him quickly.

'Whatever do you mean?'

'Well, within a couple of years they'll have finished the new airport. A charming view that'll provide, won't it? Not to mention the sound-effects.'

Hanae rose from her knees almost as smoothly and grace-fully as she had done when younger, and went over to her husband. They were both wearing nothing but lightweight *yukatas*, and when she raised both hands and put them lightly on his shoulders he could smell the familiar fragrance of her body, plumper now but still powerfully attractive to him.

'You *have* been in the dumps this evening, haven't you? Is anything the matter? At the office?' There had been a time when Otani never discussed police work with her, but that was long past.

He leant forward and kissed her gently on the forehead. 'No, nothing special. I just get depressed thinking about the way things are going in this country. Sorry to inflict my bad moods on you, though.' He straightened up and smiled. 'As it happens, I was feeling a bit down this morning and took it into my head to invite Hara out for lunch. He quite cheered me up for a while.'

'How?'

'Well, I suppose it amounted to gross flattery, really. You know I've always found him terribly boring, forever saying things like "For your added information, sir", and so on. To my great surprise, once we were in the restaurant he not only talked to me like a normal human being, but told me that in the office I make him feel inadequate. I ask you!'

'Did he say why? What? You're mumbling, say that again.'

'Oh, just some nonsense about my being pretty well known as a detective.'

Hanae flung her arms round his waist and hugged him. 'And so you are! A great detective!' Then she slipped her hands up to the base of his neck and probed the muscles there. 'And what's more, you're all knotted up. Come here, *Shaaloku Homuzuru*, and I'll give you a massage.'

'Would you? I'd like that.' Otani stretched out face downwards on the futons, let his arms flop naturally where they would and turned his head to one side. It occurred to him that while in late nineteenth-century London Sherlock Holmes might very possibly have experienced the relaxing pleasure of a massage, it would certainly not have been at the hands of a lightly clad female. He didn't pursue the train of thought, but simply surrendered to Hanae's ministrations, wincing at first from time to time when her strong fingers found one bunched muscle after another and worked at it without mercy until it gave up the struggle and settled into proper alignment.

After a while there was no discomfort; quite the reverse – his consciousness seemed to float free of his body and he was aware only of a delicious lassitude which seemed to be both physical and mental. Otani wasn't sleepy, not even drowsy, but time and space had ceased to have any meaning. The only constant was the movement of Hanae's hands, and even they seemed paradoxically disembodied.

'I wonder if this is what nirvana's like?' he managed to grunt eventually. 'Hope so.'

Hanae's hands momentarily stopped moving, but the

now gentle, smoothing strokes soon started again. 'That's a nice thing to say. Would you like me to stop now? Had enough?'

'Not really, but I feel marvellous now and you must be tired. Just lie beside me for a while. I'm too lazy even to get into bed, and besides, I've got something to tell you. It seems that Michiko might have been right about trouble at that summer school of hers.'

'Really? What's happened?'

'Well, we don't know exactly what it signifies yet, but there's been quite a bit of excitement. Kimura went there today to have a look round. Pretended to be a journalist, it seems. You must understand that I got all this from Hara. Kimura rang him from Sasayama at about five, but he'd spoken to Junko Migishima earlier. You probably remember Michiko telling me that there were two people running the summer school, what you might call the academic boss, name of Kido, and an American in charge of the administrative arrangements.'

'I remember, yes.' Hanae was now lying on her side, lazily teasing at the hair at the nape of his neck and occasionally tugging at his earlobes. 'Kido's the – what's the word – accident-prone one.'

'How right you are. Anyway, Kimura talked his way into the place easily enough as you'd expect and met Kido, who wasn't feeling too good and passed Kimura on to the American, who showed him all over the place. And do you know, within a couple of hours Kido was found in his quarters, dead.'

Hanae pulled herself up into a sitting position and gaped down at him.

'*Dead*?'

'That's right. And as matters stand, nobody has the slightest idea why. Kimura reported that in the morning there was some sort of mishap during fire drill, when Kido was demonstrating the use of an extinguisher and managed

73

to get his shirt and trousers soaking wet. And then it seems Kido went straight out of hot sunshine into an air conditioned building in his wet clothes. So not surprisingly he was shivering, and Kimura reckoned he was asking for a severe chill. But he certainly didn't expect to see the poor chap's body being carted off in an ambulance the same day.'

'A heart attack perhaps? After the shock?'

'We might know tomorrow. They're doing an autopsy. All I've been told at the moment is that Kimura smells something fishy about it. I've suggested Hara should go to Sasayama tomorrow as well, and have a confidential chat with Michiko. It's a nuisance, because he's busy enough as it is without that. Between them, Hara and Ninja Noguchi appear to have mislaid a suspected gangster.'

Hanae had slid down beside him again while he was talking, and renewed her attentions to his neck and ears. 'Well, with all this going on, I should have thought you'd be too busy to get depressed. Roll over, I'll do your other side.' Otani did so, and Hanae, now kneeling, looked down with a broad smile. 'My goodness, what's *this*?'

Then, blushing becomingly, she untied her sash and slipped out of her yukata.

Nine

While Hanae was giving Otani his massage, and later, Noguchi was eating bits and pieces of liver, kidney, chicken gizzard and other less easily identifiable kinds of offal grilled on bamboo skewers at a scruffy little snack bar not far from the main line railway station in Osaka. Other customers had come and gone, but currently he was alone with the Korean proprietor. Noguchi was taking his time over his so-called 'stamina food', ordering a couple of skewers at a time, at intervals of ten or fifteen minutes, and washing the strongly flavoured mouthfuls down with plenty of second-grade sake. The Korean served it by the glass tumbler; his regular patrons would have turned up their noses at proper sake cups.

It was easy enough to get from Kobe to Osaka, about half an hour by any of the three rival railways that served the area, but it was not a city Noguchi cared for particularly. Nevertheless he went there from time to time. He had a number of informative acquaintances in Osaka and occasionally he found it useful to consult them, often without their realising it. He had been doing just that earlier in the evening, and then indulged his periodical hankering to visit the snack-bar of his Korean friend, who was a perceptive and tactful person but not one of Noguchi's underworld informants. He was held in much higher regard than those. For in a manner of speaking he was a kind of relative, being the nephew of Noguchi's late common-law wife and therefore full cousin to his only son, now also dead.

Noguchi had never got over the loss of either of them. He would gladly have married the woman known as Mrs Lim and to hell with what people thought or said, and had often made the suggestion, but she had always refused. She had died young – of cancer after months of agony, leaving Noguchi plunged in a grief all the more harrowing because there were few who knew of it and none to whom he could open his heart.

The death of their gifted, wayward son by his own hand had been even harder to take. The young Lim had chosen during his boyhood to pronounce his surname in the Japanese way, as Hayashi, had won himself a university place and had emerged as a radical leader in the student revolts of the sixties, before fleeing to North Korea. It had been the cruellest of ironies that when the young man – now once more called Lim – had slipped back into Japan as a Korean agent it had been his own father who had unknowingly helped to trap him. Anyone who knew him could have predicted that Lim, in confinement, would use the suicide pill he had secreted on him, but the trauma had all but broken his father.

'He's just turned twelve, you know,' Noguchi suddenly said, breaking the companionable silence. The Korean nodded. He knew Noguchi was talking about the North Korean grandson of whose existence he had learned in the one poignant private conversation between father and son that Otani had broken all the rules to arrange.

'Fine lad, I'll bet. Things are changing all the time. You never know, you might get to see him one of these days.'

'And pigs might fly.' Noguchi pushed his empty tumbler forward and watched the Korean refill it from the electric sake-warmer mounted on the wooden counter, near a fly-blown Nikka whisky calendar that featured a photograph of Paul Newman raising a glass of the stuff in a toast. 'Another couple of sticks of liver and then I'll be getting along.' As usual, an hour or so in the company of his friend had cheered him up. They seldom exchanged more than a few sentences, but Noguchi always went away warmed, and not because of the sake.

'See you,' he said a few minutes later after disposing of the grilled liver and the sake. He slapped three crumpled thousand-yen notes down on the counter and pushed his way out through the divided hanging curtain which was all the bar boasted by way of a doorway at that time of the year. Noguchi always insisted on paying for his food and drink there, and always paid a little too much.

'Sure, take care of yourself,' the Korean replied.

Out in the little alleyway lined with similar cheap bars and eating-houses, many with their names painted on red or white paper lanterns, Noguchi hitched up his disgraceful old trousers and began to amble back in the general direction of the station. He was still thinking about his grandson, but no longer particularly sadly. It had occurred to him that it might be possible to get hold of a photograph of the boy by dropping a hint next time he visited the Korean. The huge Korean community in Japan was sharply divided, between those who professed allegiance to the People's Republic and those who looked to Seoul, and those on either side of the divide seemed to hate their opponents' guts almost as much as they detested almost all Japanese. But Noguchi had friends in both camps, and when it came to the point blood was thicker than water and there were lines of communication. It would be good to have a picture of the lad.

After a little while he surfaced from his reverie and became aware that a seedy-looking little man had joined him and was muttering something out of the side of his mouth. Noguchi spared him a disdainful look.

'Do I know you?' he enquired, certain that he didn't.

'No, but I know you, guv. You're Noguchi.'

'And who's he when he's at home?'

'When he's at home, he's in Kobe, and people call him Ninja.'

'Do they now? So what's up with you? Collecting auto-graphs?'

'No. Just wondering what a bit of news might be worth to you. See, I happened to be buying a packet of popcorn out of the machine in the lobby of the Sexy Cinema earlier. While you was talking to the old girl that sells the tickets. And I got interested.'

'You shouldn't waste your money in places like that,' Noguchi said to him solemnly as they turned the corner and moved into the shadows underneath the railway bridge, noisy with incessant road traffic but with few pedestrians on the sidewalk. After a few paces Noguchi stopped and faced the man. 'They never let you see anything except tits. And too much popcorn'll make you fart.'

'Yeah, but the thing is, you didn't go in and see nothing at all, not even the tits. You gave the old girl a couple of notes, but she never gave you no ticket. Five thousands, was they, or tens?'

'You want your eyes tested. I was just asking her what day they change the films. Besides, she's my grandma. All right, sunshine, what are you offering?'

'Heard you mention a name.'

'Get on with it. I haven't got all night to play games.'

'Hosoda. Bloke that put a slug into his lady friend's toy-boy and got sent down for it. Actor on the telly he was, the boy friend. It was in all the papers at the time. They let him out last week.'

'So?'

'Fifty thou for his present address.'

'Pal of his, are you? Drop in for a drink now and then?'

'Come off it, guv. Listen, this is straight up. I'll give you this for nothing. He's got a couple of big-shot pals, name of Takeuchi and Ikeda. They know where he is, and so do I. You could ask them, but I reckon it'd be quicker and easier to slip me the fif—'

Such was the racket under the bridge that Noguchi didn't

even recognise the shots as such. Even if he had, he couldn't possibly have seen which of the stream of cars and taxis sweeping by a yard or two away had carried the gunman. He did see the look in the little man's eyes just before he crumpled. It was one of slightly pained surprise. He looked as if his last thought might well have been that he had been cheated out of his fifty thousand yen.

*

'The cheek of the bastards! Practically just across the street from HQ!' The night duty inspector at Osaka Prefectural Police Headquarters was simultaneously outraged and excited. Excited because so far as he knew this was the first time that the legendary Ninja Noguchi had set foot in the building, and outraged by the thought that he might well return to his base in Kobe and put it about that the Osaka lot permitted gangland shootings to take place more or less outside their front doors.

It was fortunate for Noguchi that this particular inspector was an admirer of his and that his name had come up on the duty list for that night; for Noguchi had experienced a bad fifteen minutes before turning up on his doorstep. A good number of pedestrians, assuming that it was a couple of drunks impeding their path, had skirted round them with averted faces while he was checking that his would-be informant was in fact dead. Others quickened their steps and hurried past in horror when Noguchi stood up with blood all over his hands and sleeves and started bellowing for someone to fetch a policeman. When that did no good Noguchi simply walked out into the flow of traffic, held up his hand and brought the first car he encountered to a halt with a screeching of tyres, followed almost immediately by a resounding clang and tinkling of glass as the car behind ran into it.

That had brought a policeman on the scene quickly enough. The drivers of the two cars involved in the collision immediately tried to claim his attention, which he seemed disposed to give them after first using his walkie-talkie to report the incident and summon help. Noguchi, righteously indignant at being ignored, grabbed the officer by the lapels, forcibly twisted him round and bent him over the body on the ground. The policeman didn't like this at all, nor did he like the look of the fat but powerful elderly man with cropped hair who smelt strongly of sake, whose clothes were not only disreputable but had bloodstains on them, yet who claimed to be a senior police officer from the neighbouring Hyogo force.

'Yeah, right. Sorry it happened on your patch.' Cleaned up after a fashion, Noguchi was slumped in a chair which, surprisingly, was big enough to accommodate him, and thinking hard while doing his best to humour the keen young inspector. He had waved away the inevitable green tea brought for him, but accepted the offer of a police car to take him back to Kobe.

'Well, writing this up'll certainly make a change from the sort of report I generally turn in.'

'Hold your horses, son. Don't want to spoil your fun, but I'd appreciate it if you'd be a bit careful what you say. Got to report the crash of course – dozens of witnesses anyway. And picking up and carting off the stiff. But leave me out of it for the time being, okay?' Noguchi raised a hand when he saw the crestfallen look in the inspector's eye and treated him to a conspiratorial wink. 'Undercover assignment, know what I mean? My boss'll be in touch with your commander first thing in the morning, and I can promise you he'll be giving you a good chit. I'd've been in a right pickle without your help, and I won't forget to say so.'

The Osaka man nodded, eyes wide.

'Now, about the stiff – I haven't got a clue who he is. I took him for a tout when he came up to me, but he knew who I was. Wanted to sell me some info but didn't have time to get round to saying what it was, so he must've been some kind of nark. My advice to you is to pass that little lot to your CID and let them get on with it. We'll keep in touch with them.'

'Whatever you say, Inspector Noguchi. Very proud to be of assistance.'

'You'll go a long way, son. No need to overdo the flannel, though.' He yawned horribly. 'Take you up on that car ride now if you don't mind. Been a busy evening. I'll just make a quick phone call first.'

Fifteen minutes later Noguchi was sprawled in the back of an Osaka police car, bowling along the Hanshin Highway Number Two on the way back to Kobe and a late evening conference with Hara at his flat. Their little girl would have long since been put to bed, which was a pity, but she'd got to have her sleep.

He wondered how long it would take the Osaka lot to identify the corpse now in their official charge in the mortuary. They'd get there in the end, but it could be a longish job for them. Noguchi sighed loudly for the benefit of the driver, shifted his position and in the process took out the tatty wallet he had removed from the dead man's hip pocket while examining him. There wasn't enough light in the car to read by, but it looked as if there were enough bits and pieces of paper and plastic inside the wallet for Hara to have the little nark's life history printed out and on his desk by morning.

He told the driver where to let him off when they got to Kobe, and settled down for a little nap in the meantime.

Ten

Having always hitherto reckoned his colleague Hara to be among the most punctilious of men, Kimura was surprised not to find him already there when he arrived at the little police station in Sasayama the next morning at nine-thirty as agreed over the telephone early the previous evening. Kimura himself had toyed with and abandoned the idea of staying overnight in the town rather than going back to Kobe, and trying to persuade Philippa Kilpeck to have dinner with him.

Her manner on leaving him the previous afternoon had after all been distinctly chilly. Kimura had – with good reason – unruffled faith in his power to charm the ladies, but he was sensitive enough to accept that she was deeply upset over the sudden death of Professor Kido. So even in the unlikely event of her agreeing to meet him off the summer school premises it was hardly to be supposed that it would have been in a state of mind conducive to social chit-chat, much less the gently flirtatious conversational skirmishing he had in mind.

Kimura had therefore done the sensible thing and gone back to his comfortable bachelor flat, from which he had rung Hara at home for a further discussion and learned of Otani's 'suggestion' that Hara should himself go to Anraku-in the next day and interview Michiko Yanagida in confidence. He saw the logic in that. Unless and until the pathological examination provided some evidence that Kido's death was not from natural causes, there was nothing

83

for the police to investigate officially, and there could be advantages in Kimura's maintaining his pose as a journalist. It could indeed still quite possibly turn out that they had all been wasting their time and that Otani's sister-in-law had been imagining things.

While waiting for Hara, Kimura whiled away the time by chatting to the middle-aged sergeant in charge of the police station, whose manner towards a senior officer was scrupulously correct but who at first clearly viewed his nattily dressed, citified visitor as an effete popinjay who couldn't be expected to know which end was up. Kimura was used to this sort of attitude, and soon drew the older man out on the subject of foreigners, contributing only the odd sage comment of his own. By the time Hara did turn up, twenty minutes late and full of apologies, Kimura and the sergeant were getting along like a house on fire.

As soon as the sergeant had bustled off to organise refreshments, leaving his two VIPs in possession of the tiny office, Kimura turned to his colleague with raised eyebrows. 'Are you all right? You look a bit rough. Been out on the tiles?'

Hara managed a wan smile. 'I wish I could surprise you by saying yes, but I'm feeling nothing more than the effects of a late night and a very early start. Ninja Noguchi was at my place until after one, and what he told me meant I had to put in a couple of hours at the office before I set out to come here.'

'Tell me more.'

'Of course. After we've dealt with the matter in hand. I managed to get hold of Professor Yanagida on the phone, and I'm to meet her at a coffee shop not far from Anraku-in at eleven. We might go there together – ah, Sergeant, there you are! Thank you so much. You will join us, of course.'

Unlike Kimura and in spite of being only in his mid-thirties, Hara looked every inch the responsible official. The day was already sultry, but he was wearing a necktie as sombre as his suit, and lack of sleep had given him an appropriately harassed look. There was barely room for the three of them in the office, but the sergeant squeezed himself in with his tray. Kimura disapproved of instant coffee on principle but took his mugful with good grace and sipped it as it was, while Hara and their host added spoonfuls of sugar from a cracked bowl to theirs, and 'Creap' brand powdered whitener from the jar.

The civilities disposed of, there was very little the two headquarters men needed to discuss with the sergeant, beyond underlining the necessity for him to maintain total discretion about their interest in the death of Professor Kido, and if necessary and until otherwise instructed to support Kimura's cover story. It became clear in any case that Junko Migishima had done a good job on him the previous day, contriving, it appeared, to leave him with the impression that the autopsy report – due to be picked up from the district general hospital later that morning – was to be treated much as if it were a state secret. When the subject was raised, the sergeant solemnly undertook to collect the document himself and keep it on his person until he handed it unopened to Hara, who would call in again at the police station before returning to Kobe.

The official Sasayama log-book showed that a telephone call had been received from the summer school secretary Shoko Yasuda some fifteen minutes after Hara had been contacted by Junko Migishima. Miss Yasuda, speaking on behalf of the American co-director Mr Ashley and sounding greatly distressed, had wanted advice about contacting Professor Kido's family. Having read out his home address and telephone number, she had been told that the police would take care of things. The sergeant had then very properly confirmed by means of phone calls to the ambulance service and the hospital that Kido was in fact dead.

'And after that you called my office and duly reported all this to Woman Senior Detective Migishima. Excellent,

Sergeant. It is clear to me that everything is being handled at this end with exemplary efficiency,' Hara said gravely. 'As you already know, the late Professor Kido lived in Akashi just west of Kobe, and I can reassure you that a message was at once passed to our divisional headquarters there, instructing the duty officer to send the patrolman from the neighbourhood police box to convey the sad news to Mrs Kido. She was at home, it seems, and, naturally, acquainted with the patrolman, who did his best to break it gently. It is always best for the local man to handle such disagreeable tasks if possible.'

*

'The widow will have to be given some explanation if it turns out that we can't release the body to her right away,' Kimura said after they had left the police station and were strolling in the direction of Anraku-in. With time in hand they had agreed to walk together at least part of the way.

'True, but that all depends on the pathologist's findings. Tell me, what is your impression of Professor Yanagida?'

Kimura grinned. 'Want to know what you're in for, do you? Can't say I blame you. I've never actually met her, of course. If I had, I couldn't have spent a good bit of yesterday wandering about the place and likely to bump into her at any minute. But I've seen her in action, at an international student society goodwill party in Kyoto that turned into a punch-up. I'm not a bit surprised she's involved in this project. Very hot on international understanding, is the Chief's sister-in-law.'

'So I believe. She must also be very able, to have become a full professor at a national university. There still aren't more than a handful of women in those posts in the country.'

'Must be brainy all right, but you'll be a better judge of that than me. I can tell you one thing, she's a very different sort of woman from her elder sister. You're going to have your work cut out, Hara. Unmarried, as you know, and a few years ago at least she used to make herself look a bit ridiculous by dressing up like the kids in her classes. A fairly militant feminist – dislikes men on principle.'

'If I were a Japanese woman I expect I would too,' Hara said with an innocent sideways glance at Kimura. 'So Professor Yanagida has a strong personality. Is it a stable one, would you say? If it hadn't been for her approaching the commander, neither of us would be here and Kido's death would have been treated as just another statistic.'

'You're supposed to be the detective around here, make the obvious deduction. She's the chief's wife's *sister* for heaven's sake. Can you see him putting us on to this if he thought she was given to paranoia? And besides, I told you on the phone there's definitely something odd going on there. The secretary reacted very strangely when I asked to meet Kido. May have been afraid I was an assassin come to get him, for all I know.' A thought struck him. 'I say, Hara, the poor guy died a couple of hours after I turned up. Maybe she thinks I *am* a killer!'

'If Miss Yasuda does accuse you and can produce any evidence to support her suspicions, I can assure you that I shall examine it with special care.'

'Really, Hara, I said that by way of a joke!'

'So did I.'

'Oh, did you? I'd never have guessed. Anyway, listen, what about the Australian woman? I told you what she said when they carted Kido's body away.'

Hara and Kimura walked on together for a further fifteen minutes or so, during which time Hara explained the reason for Noguchi's late call at the Hara apartment, and retailed Noguchi's own account of his eventful evening in Osaka. Kimura was interested enough in it purely as a story, but since it appeared to have nothing whatever to do with foreigners he let much of the detail wash over him.

The wallet Noguchi had removed from the would-be

informer's pocket had yielded quite enough to identify its owner as Tomoaki Miyamoto, aged forty-seven, a street-cleaner employed by the Osaka municipal authorities. Kimura gathered that for reasons of their own Noguchi and Hara had agreed to leave the Osaka prefectural police to figure that out for themselves, at least until after Otani had spoken to his opposite number in the neighbouring force.

After coming to the end of his account, Hara hailed a taxi to take him to the coffee shop where he was to meet Michiko Yanagida, and Kimura, having agreed to rendez-vous with him again at Sasayama railway station at one p.m., waited for a bus. When one came along he boarded it but got off at the stop before Anraku-in, and went into a photographic supply shop which like most such places in Japan had a large painted sign outside bearing simply the three roman capital letters 'DPE', each in a different colour. Few people if asked could have said they stood for the English term 'Developing, Printing and Enlarging', for over the years '*dii-pii-ii*' had become as thoroughly Japanese a word as '*kamera*' and '*firumu*'. Kimura had dropped his own exposed film in there on finally leaving Anraku-in the previous afternoon, and his prints were ready to be picked up.

He flipped through them outside the shop. The quality wasn't anything special, but the idiot-proof camera had ensured good, clear images. Whether or not they would reward careful scrutiny he couldn't at this stage say, but he was glad he had taken them.

Arriving at Anraku-in, Kimura made his way quietly to the closed door of the summer school office in the impressive main building and listened. The unmistakeable voice and accent of Bill Ashley speaking in Japanese was just audible, but Kimura couldn't make out any distinct words. Kimura tapped on the door, opened it right away and glanced inside. He was quick enough to see Shoko Yasuda quickly dash the back of her hand across her eyes and bend over her typewriter, as Bill Ashley straightened up. Ashley had been leaning over the secretary's desk supporting himself on his two fists, and judging by his expression had either been berating the young woman about something or reasoning with her. He made no attempt to disguise his displeasure at the sight of Kimura.

'God, are you still here? Look, I—'

'Please, I only looked in to express my sincere condolences.'

Ashley took in Kimura's apologetic smile and then glanced at his hands, raised in something between apology and benediction, and grunted something incomprehensible.

'It's just that you and Miss Yasuda here were so helpful yesterday, and I felt bad about not having a chance in all the confusion to say thank you and make my farewells.'

'Yeah. Well, okay, you're welcome. Sorry I snapped at you, but you'll understand we have quite a lot on our minds just now.'

'Sure. I'll get out of your hair right away. I take it the summer school will go ahead?'

'Of course it will. Send us a copy of your article when it comes out. Okay? Right, so long.'

After thanking the silent and puffy-eyed Miss Yasuda profusely in Japanese and bestowing a final look of kindly concern on Ashley, Kimura left the room. He doubted if Ashley was interested enough in him to make sure that he really did leave the premises right away. Anyway, if challenged he could perfectly well point out that he hadn't said he was going to – merely that he wouldn't bother Ashley or Miss Yasuda again.

The emergency exit at the end of the corridor was still unlocked, and Kimura wandered once more out past the classroom block and into the open space where he had first set eyes on the hapless Professor Kido. There were a few people about, but nobody he could remember having met the previous day, and none who paid any attention to him as he drifted apparently aimlessly in the direction of the bungalow-like residential buildings.

Arriving at the entrance of the nearest one, Kimura saw that the lobby was slightly raised. It was floored with highly polished dove-grey vinyl tiles, but a scatter of shoes on the lower level and a neat row of backless green plastic slippers on the step indicated that people were nevertheless expected to observe traditional Japanese practice and leave their outdoor footwear there.

The entire furniture of the lobby consisted of a stiff arrangement of two diminutive easy-chairs, a matching sofa and a low coffee table. The seats were upholstered in simulated leather, the table made of simulated walnut. So far as Kimura could judge, the lobby and everything in it was artificial. Corridors led off from either side.

At least his own shoes were of the finest hand-crafted Italian leather. He slipped them off, stepped up into a pair of the plastic flip-flops, took a hundred-yen coin out of his pocket and spun it. Numerals, turn left, flowers, right. It came down with the flower design uppermost, and Kimura began to walk along the corridor the coin had told him to. The first three doors he passed bore names on cards in little frames. Manfred Weisse occupied the first room, Howard Bayliss the second, and a Japanese the third. The name meant nothing to Kimura – one of the lecturers presumably. Next came a group of washrooms and toilets clearly labelled for the use of men only, and the remaining doors further down the corridor were obviously those to three more study-bedrooms.

On an impulse, Kimura went back to the lobby and through into the other corridor, wondering if the Anraku-in authorities were sufficiently enlightened to house women and men under the same roof. They were. The layout was identical to that on the other side, except that the toilet facilities were labelled 'WOMEN'. The first three bedrooms were allotted to Ms Margaret Threlfall, Ms Inger

Lindblad, and Prof. Michiko Yanagida respectively – and the first one beyond the washrooms to Dr Philippa Kilpeck.

Who opened her door from inside while Kimura was gazing at it speculatively, and responded to his sheepish smile with a frozen lift of her eyebrows.

'What, may I ask, do you think you're doing?' she enquired. 'And incidentally, just who the dickens *are* you?'

Eleven

'Asphyxiated, eh?' Otani had read the autopsy report through twice, and now took off his reading glasses and looked up, the report balanced on his knee. The four of them were in their usual chairs in his office. Thirty-six hours after his adventure in Osaka, Noguchi looked none the worse for it; but since his normal appearance was so dilapidated it was hard to be sure. Hara had caught up to some extent on his lost sleep but still had dark circles under his eyes, while Kimura was his usual jaunty self. 'Interesting that the local pathologist thought it advisable to get a second opinion from his old professor at Kyoto University Hospital.'

'He had been warned by us through the Sasayama police to take particular care, sir. In the ordinary way he could perhaps have been forgiven if he had attributed the death to a heart attack. The anomalies – blood oxygen level, and so on – seem to have been barely perceptible.'

'So the report makes clear. But how was it done, Hara? No marks on the face, no fibres, traces of feather or what have you in the nasal tract. Any ideas?'

'None as yet, sir. The very faint bruising round the wrists suggest that the victim might have been held down, but equally that no great pressure was required.'

'He had taken a couple of codeines beforehand,' Kimura pointed out. 'As the autopsy report mentions. I'm not in the least surprised, having seen how groggy he looked after drenching himself and then sitting about in that arctic air conditioning. By the time he got himself into bed he was probably pretty dopy. Wouldn't have put up much of a struggle.'

'You say you picked up this report at the Sasayama police station after you'd finished with my sister-in-law, read it, met Kimura as agreed at one and discussed it with him.'

'That's right, Chief. We decided urgent action was called for, so Hara and I collected a uniformed man and rushed straight back to Anraku-in with the idea of sealing Kido's room. We realised it was probably too late, but—'

'But you got lucky, because this bright girl, what's her name, Yasuda, had done your work for you.'

'Precisely. Nipped into the room right after the ambulance men took Kido away, put all his stuff in plastic bags and stowed it away somewhere. Including the sheets and pillow-case off his bed. They're now at the regional forensic lab, along with the fire extinguisher. She'd put that to one side, too, in case it had been doped somehow. A very long shot, but worth looking at.'

'Smart girl,' Otani commented. 'Why isn't she in the police? Maybe we should give her a recruitment booklet.'

'Mrs Migishima might talk her into it. She's already had one long session with her.' It wasn't much of a joke, but coming from Hara it was a surprise, and was followed by a few moments of general relaxation and shifting in chairs.

'All right. We'll come to Detective Migishima's interview report in a minute. Evidently the young woman had her suspicions, and Kimura was right to notice something odd about her manner earlier that day. Before we get to that, let me just get the sequence of events clear in my own mind,' Otani said then. 'You first, Hara. How did you get on with my sister-in-law? You didn't at that stage know that Kido had been murdered.'

'Professor Yanagida is a most impressive lady, sir. And, if I may say so, a very beautiful one.' If Hara's little witticism had rung the bell, this gallant remark caused a minor sensation. Kimura whooped with pleasure, and Noguchi's barrel chest heaved.

The muscles round Otani's mouth twitched, but when he spoke it was in mildly enquiring tones. 'You were smitten with her?'

Hara forged ahead, doggedly but with a touch of colour in his cheeks. 'Of course not, sir. I did, however, form a most favourable impression of the professor as an entirely credible, ah, informant. Manifestly she is a highly intelligent and educated lady, an intellectual and a scholar. These characteristics and qualities do not invariably preclude either gullibility or a lively and perhaps unreliable imagination; but I am convinced that Professor Yanagida is a clear-sighted, level-headed person, and I trust her judgment.'

'In short, you liked her and you think her ideas should be taken seriously.'

'I do, sir, and I should like to stress that hindsight has nothing to do with that opinion. The professor described concisely and clearly the two incidents involving Professor Kido that she had witnessed: the collapse of a massive roof-beam within inches of his head during a visit to a Shinto shrine, and an arrow flying through the open window of the common-room and just missing Kido when only he, Professor Yanagida and an Australian summer-school participant were inside.'

'That arrow business couldn't possibly have been an accident, could it?'

'Professor Yanagida agrees, sir, and was puzzled at the time by Kido's reaction. He made no attempt to go in search of the culprit. If I may continue, she has also provided informative character sketches of the leading personalities among the members of the summer school, in the form of written notes, which I have had word-processed.' Hara picked up the neat folder which he had placed on the floor beside his chair, opened it and handed photocopies of a two-page document to Otani and Kimura, Noguchi having shaken his head in refusal.

Otani glanced through the sheets in a few seconds. 'Might turn out to be useful. I'll study it later. We shall need a full list of everybody at that place anyway. What did she have to say about Kido's death? In view of the previous near misses, had she jumped to the conclusion that there must be something fishy about it?'

'No, sir. It would have been understandable had she done so, but Professor Yanagida was scrupulous to avoid taking anything for granted. She naturally and rightly assumed that the cause of death would be the subject of careful investigation.'

'Did she mention the remark Kimura heard the Australian woman make? Let me just have a look at what she wrote about her . . . I'll read it out: "Threlfall, Margaret. Australian high-school teacher of Japanese, probably about fifty years of age. Divorced, no children. Frequently in the company of William Ashley, with whom she seems to be extremely friendly. Competent command of spoken Japanese, can read and comprehend a daily newspaper with frequent recourse to a dictionary. Noisy, outspoken and opinionated, clearly regarded Professor Kido as something of a figure of fun, but a shrewd observer of people. When it became obvious that Kido had passed away, publicly implied, in English, that he had been murdered; but this could possibly have been an attempt at a joke, in characteristically bad taste." Well, well. My sister-in-law seems to be a pretty shrewd observer of people herself. I'd hate to read her on the subject of me.'

'Yes, sir.'

Otani darted a suspicious glance at Hara. The remark in itself was meaningless, but it occurred to him that if Michiko had during their tête-à-tête in the coffee shop been moved to offer any views about her sister's husband, Hara would certainly have listened attentively. Maybe that was why he had been speaking so highly of her intellectual powers and judgment.

'She must have been surprised if she saw you turning up at Anraku-in with Kimura and a patrolman in uniform an hour or so after you'd parted the best of friends,' he said a little sourly, then turned to Kimura. 'Which brings us to you. You had quite a bit of explaining to do.'

'Well, yes and no, Chief.' Otani thought he looked distinctly shifty, and waited patiently for him to explain himself.

'I think Ashley was genuinely astonished when Hara and I walked in on him and identified ourselves as police officers investigating the circumstances of Kido's death. So was the secretary, Shoko Yasuda – the look of relief on her face ought to be reported as a piece of evidence in itself. But I, er, that is, I'm afraid one of the foreign participants I'd been talking to had already come to the conclusion that I wasn't what I'd claimed to be.'

'What's her name?' Otani asked, in no doubt whatever that it must have been a woman and turning his attention again to his copy of Michiko's notes.

'Dr Philippa Kilpeck.'

'And how did she see through you?'

'It was my camera, I'm afraid. I'm no photographer as you know, so I've got one of these automatic ones that does everything for you. Dr Kilpeck has an identical model that she bought in London for under fifty pounds – say about twelve or thirteen thousand yen.'

'And she quite rightly decided the *Kobe Shimbun* would expect its contributors to invest in better quality equipment. I see. Ah, here she is. "Kilpeck, Philippa. British, medieval historian, single, late thirties. Holds doctorate from London University. A sound scholar who has published a good deal. Specialist in fifteenth-century English history, but extremely well informed about parallel events in medieval Japan, notably the Onin War. Previously acquainted with Professor Kido, of whom she speaks with respect and admiration. Blonde, attractive, elegantly groomed, she is charming and courteous in manner but gives the impression of being self-contained and of an observant habit of mind" – spotted your cheap camera, didn't she, Kimura – "has learned a few everyday Japanese expressions but has not studied the language . . ." et cetera, et cetera.'

'The maddening thing,' Kimura said, still nursing a grievance, 'is that I had to pay twenty thousand for that camera here in Japan. I can't understand it.'

'Never mind that. So this blonde historian saw through you more or less right away.'

'I'm afraid so. And when she taxed me with it I had no option but to come clean. Because unfortunately I was snooping around in one of the residential buildings at the time and she caught me. This was day two, of course, and I was back again with Hara.'

'*In propria persona*,' Hara put in, and then, seeing nothing but blank looks: 'Latin. As Inspector Kimura, I mean. Within an hour or so of having been unmasked by the English lady, sir. So no great harm done.'

Otani shook his head at Kimura in mock despair. 'All right, I accept that. And on the whole I approve the steps you've both taken. I think I shall pay a visit to Anraku-in myself in a day or two and take a look round. They're going ahead with the summer school in spite of all this, are they?'

'Yes, sir. Fortunately for us, because it means that all the people concerned will be available for questioning for another week if necessary, rather than dispersing all over the place. Notably the foreigners, or course. Mrs Migishima is staying on the premises until she has statements from all the Japanese women, and between us Inspector Kimura and I will cover all the men with whatever help we find necessary.'

Otani sighed and turned to Noguchi. 'Well, Ninja. Do *you* happen to know how to asphyxiate a man and leave no mark on his face?'

'Ask me another.'

'I will. You've listened patiently to all that, and

presumably agree that Kimura and Hara have got their work cut out for the next few days at least. So what are we going to do about this fellow Miyamoto who managed to get himself shot in your company outside my Osaka colleague's HQ?'

Noguchi, assuming that if he waited long enough Otani would tell him, did so.

'We're going to have to sort it out between us, that's what. As you know but the others may not, my opposite number there was very good about it all when I spoke to him yesterday morning. Ninja won't be stuck for the cost of repairs to the two cars he made collide. Or be charged mileage for the ride back to Kobe in their car. The least I could do in return was to pretend not to know it already when he called me back late in the afternoon to tell me they thought they could put a name to the corpse. Conveniently enough, the late Miyamoto lived just this side of the prefectural line, so we can have him. What's the matter now, Kimura? Still annoyed about being overcharged for your camera?'

'No, it's just that one of the instructors at the summer school's called Miyamoto. Pottery, or maybe paper-making. Can't remember. Bit of a coincidence.'

'No it isn't. There are thousands of Miyamotos. Not quite as bad as Suzuki but not far off. So you and Hara go off and have a word with your gaggle of intellectuals, and leave Ninja and me with our deceased Osaka garbage man and small-time nark.'

Twelve

'You should see this place in April when the cherry blossom's at its best,' Kimura said, pausing for a moment to take in the scene in Maruyama Park. 'It's almost like carnival time in the south of France.'

As a matter of fact there was plenty going on around them that Saturday afternoon in Kyoto, at the height of the summer holiday season. The rustic-style restaurants and tea-houses were doing brisk business, with mounds of shaved ice topped with highly coloured syrup being particularly popular with the children while their elders sat on benches in the shade drinking beer or Seven-Up. Some distance away Japanese tour-groups were obediently arranging themselves in rows at the behest of their uniformed, white gloved 'bus-girl' guides to have their photographs taken against the backdrop of the looming facade of the great Chion-in Temple. Here and there westerners in holiday garb wandered about, mostly in couples, some exclaiming from time to time in delight, others looking hot and slightly bemused.

'You know, I really am sorry I had to deceive you.'

The calm eyes shaded by the wide-brimmed straw hat surveyed him. 'That's about the fourth time you've said that today. May I once and for all point out that your journalistic pose may have taken in Bill Ashley, but that I found it singularly unconvincing almost from the first?'

In spite of the heat of the day Philippa Kilpeck looked cool and stylish in an open cotton jacket over a sleeveless silk top and loose trousers. She had changed her hat band, which was now the same oyster colour as her clothes, and wore a string of pearls round her neck. This time, however, she was wearing low-heeled shoes that made her seem much smaller than before, and more vulnerable.

'Having said that,' she went on thoughtfully, 'I must admit that I should never have guessed that you were a police officer. It's just as well that you had the impressive Inspector Hara to vouch for you when you came back in the afternoon. Until then I had very serious doubts about you.'

'I did explain how I came to be in one of the residential blocks. I had no idea it was the one you were staying in, until I saw your name on the door.'

'That scarcely accounts for the fact that you appeared to have settled down to stare at it for some time when I surprised you. Or why you invited me to accompany you to Kyoto. I should have been perfectly willing to answer your questions at Anraku-in.'

'I'm sure you would. But it was just a forty-five minute bus ride, I know you're interested in Kyoto, and darn it, it *is* Saturday afternoon. What about a cup of tea or coffee?'

They had been in each other's company already for nearly two hours and Kimura thought that even the poised Dr Kilpeck might be glad to visit a ladies' room. He was good like that.

'Thank you, I should like that.'

Kimura led the way to a gloomy-looking western-style building tucked away in a corner of the park. 'This is a more interesting place than you might guess to look at it.'

'It *looks* vaguely like the sort of house a rich late Victorian or Edwardian professional man might have lived in. In England, I mean. Whatever is it?'

'The Kyoto Ladies' Hotel.'

'A ladies' hotel? How extraordinary.'

'There are still quite a few here and there in Japan. The coffee room is through this side entrance. I think they only

use the main one nowadays for big receptions and so on.'
Once inside, Kimura discreetly pointed out the way to the
restrooms, made quick use of the men's, and was hovering in
the opulent reception area when Dr Kilpeck returned.

'It's fantastic!' she exclaimed with the first broad, open
smile of pleasure he had seen on her face. 'All these marvellous marble statues everywhere, and that *staircase*! Who on
earth owns it?'

'I'm not sure. The Kyoto city council, I think. It still func-
tions as a hotel for women only, but I can't think who'd want
to stay here.'

'I certainly would, for one.'

The nondescript modern decor of the coffee shop con-
trasted dismally with the splendours of the public rooms,
which could only be glimpsed since they were not open to
non-residents. All the same, Philippa Kilpeck's manner
remained animated and even friendly after they were seated
and had been provided with lemon tea and strawberry short-
cake.

'You said you've visited Kyoto two or three times before
since you arrived in Japan,' Kimura said.

'Yes. It was the first stop on the organised tour for all the
summer school people, not surprisingly. Not a huge success,
so far as the non-Japanese were concerned.'

'Oh? Why was that?'

'We must have seemed hopelessly undisciplined and
inattentive. The fact is, most of us have very specific interests,
and a certain amount of expertise. We weren't happy being
shepherded round and lectured at like a lot of schoolchildren
or tourists, and kept wandering off in various directions.
Frankly, I can't imagine why Professor Leclerc bothered to
come at all. He's seen it all dozens of times, and he hates
having to listen to people talking English.' Then it was as if a
cloud shadowed her expression. 'It wasn't all that far from
Kyoto that poor Professor Kido had his accident.'

'Accident?'

'Yes. Actually, it was on the other side of Mount Hiei, at a famous old Shinto shrine.' She closed her eyes for a moment, trying to remember the name. 'Hiyoshi Taisha. Yes. I remember thinking it sounded like "he or she". A huge, sprawling place not far from Lake Biwa.'

'I've heard of it. Never been there. What happened?'

'We all left the bus together of course, and Professor Kido and Bill Ashley tried to keep us in a group, but it was hopeless and within five minutes most people had simply taken off to explore on their own. If you haven't been there it's hard to describe, but the various shrine buildings are scattered all over the place, more or less merging into the forest. I and one or two of the others stayed with Ashley and Professor Kido, and we were the only ones who saw what happened. It was frightening. We'd just arrived at an isolated subordinate shrine and Professor Kido was explaining the technique of its construction. He scarcely touched one of the supporting pillars and a massive roof timber crashed down and missed him by inches. I'm ashamed to say that our first reaction was of horror at the damage to a historic building. Then of course we saw that the poor man was trembling with shock and tried to get him to go back to the bus. But he absolutely refused, and later on made light of it.'

'Professor Yanagida was with you on that occasion?'

'She was certainly at Hiyoshi Taisha, yes. She didn't come on the whole tour with us, but I was very fortunate, because a day or two later she and Professor Kido brought me to Kyoto by myself to show me some of the places I'm specially interested in. She's a modern historian, of course, but a mine of information, especially about important women in Japanese history.'

'I expect you know a lot more about Kyoto than I do,' Kimura said, just to be polite.

'Yes, I'm sure I do.' She smiled at his dumbfounded expression, and went on to soften the impact of her words.

'About its past, anyway. I don't mean to be impolite, but I am a professional historian, and there are some interesting parallels between what was happening in Kyoto just over five hundred years ago and what was going on at the same time in England.'

'Would that have been the Onin War?' Kimura enquired. It was very much a shot in the dark. He had no interest in history and if he had ever been told anything about the Onin War as a boy must have promptly forgotten it again. The phrase had meant nothing to him when it cropped up in his copy of Professor Yanagida's penportraits of leading participants in the summer school, but her note on her English colleague was fresh in his mind. He was delighted when Dr Kilpeck looked startled, and leant forward keenly. 'And in England, of course . . .'

'The Wars of the Roses, yes,' she obligingly volunteered, and Kimura nodded sagely. He had never heard of that conflict either, but the name made him think again of carnival time nearly twenty years earlier on the French Riviera, and a delightful episode with a girl who initiated the acquaintance by winking at him from one of the flower-bedecked processional floats.

'It was Professor Yanagida who pointed out that the Lady Tomiyo – the wife of the Shogun Yoshimasa, of course – played a remarkably similar political role here after the birth of her son in 1464 to that of Margaret of Anjou in England after her son by Henry the Sixth had been born ten years earlier. Two extremely formidable women, and near-contemporaries.'

'Absolutely,' Kimura agreed, paralysed by boredom, and took a sip of tea. 'By the way, did you know that her sister's married to my boss?'

Wrenched unwillingly back to the late twentieth century and at first uncomprehending, his companion blinked. 'I beg your pardon?'

'My boss's wife is Professor Yanagida's sister.'

'Really.' She sounded supremely uninterested.

'Yes. And strictly between ourselves, that's why I showed up in Sasayama in the first place that day. I was planning to go to Anraku-in anyway when I saw you at the bus stop.'

'I'm not sure if I've understood you. Did you say that Professor Yanagida asked you to visit the summer school?'

'Well, not exactly. Look, this really is confidential, so please keep it to yourself. Professor Yanagida came to the conclusion that something funny was going on there. Specifically, that she was worried about the director, Kido. Somebody seemed to have it in for him. She didn't have a lot to go on – maybe she had in mind the accident at Hiyoshi Taisha you were just describing, which is why I asked if she was with you at the time. Anyhow, it bothered her enough for her to talk to my boss about it on a personal basis, and he asked me to take a quiet unofficial look round the summer school. Then, when Kido died so suddenly, it looked as if Ms Yanagida might possibly have been right, so the Chief – his name's Superintendent Otani, by the way – sent Inspector Hara to interview her officially. Wouldn't have been proper for him to do it himself, being family. And I was still under cover, of course.' He treated her to a roguish smile. 'Except that I hadn't fooled you.'

'And now you and your colleagues are interviewing everybody at the summer school. So manifestly you have good grounds to think that Professor Yanagida *was* right.'

'I'm afraid so. Would you like more tea to go with the rest of that cake?'

'Oh. No, no thank you. It's delicious, but I don't think I can manage any more. I'm ready to leave, if you are. Thank you very much, this is a fascinating building and I'm glad to have seen it.'

'Where would you like to go now?'

'I'm sorry, I really don't know . . . the Silver Pavilion, perhaps, if there's time? I can't remember the Japanese name.'

'Ginkaku-ji,' Kimura said at once. He might not know

any Japanese history, but he knew his way round the most popular sightseeing spots in Kyoto. 'We'll take a cab, it's much too far to walk on a day like this.'

'Yoshimasa picked out the site before the Onin War began. He could scarcely have foreseen ten years of conflict leaving Kyoto in ruins, a ghost city.'

'I guess not.'

'All the same he went ahead with the project, had the villa built and finally went to live there twenty years after he'd first thought of it.'

'I'll be darned.'

Philippa cast him a look of deep suspicion, but said nothing more until they reached the west exit to the park and Kimura hailed a taxi. When they were in it and on the way to the Silver Pavilion she broke the silence, sounding apologetic. 'I do realise it's unreasonable for me to expect you to share my interests and enthusiasms. You're concerned with what happened to Professor Kido. I didn't know him for long or very well, but he was kind to me, and if there was something suspicious about his death I should like to do anything I can to help you get to the bottom of it.'

'Thank you, Dr Kilpeck.'

'What I mean is that it's kind of you to escort me today, but I know you have a job to do, and questions to ask.'

'I do indeed. Will you believe me if I say that I also enjoy your company?'

She looked at him intently and in silence for a few moments, much to the satisfaction of the taxi driver who was glancing into his rear-view mirror much more frequently than was strictly necessary. A keen listener to the BBC World Service, he understood English very well, and was riveted by the talk of a suspicious death. The fact that his two passengers were, in his expert judgment, also more than a little attracted to each other was an added bonus.

*

About half an hour later, the curious taxi driver having long been paid off and taken his speculations to another part of Kyoto, Kimura and Dr Kilpeck were sitting side by side on the edge of the wooden balcony of one of the two structures which were all that was left of the medieval Shogun's elegant retirement home, their feet dangling a few inches above the ground.

A stream of other visitors passing immediately in front of them from right to left along the approved route which would take them round the mossy garden impeded their view, but not so badly as to obscure the huge truncated cone of silver sand that reared up from ground level a few yards in front of them and to their right. Some ten yards behind that, the small but exquisitely graceful two-storey Silver Pavilion itself rose up against a grove of trees.

'The sand is shaped so perfectly symmetrically that it looks unreal, doesn't? One wonders why it doesn't all slide away.'

Kimura nodded agreement and studied his copy of the leaflet they had each been given when he paid for their admission. 'It seems that people could sit over there in the pavilion and watch the moon come up and glimmer on the sand. It was supposed to look like Mount Fuji, but I don't see much resemblance myself. I wonder how many tons of sand there are there. Ten, twenty?'

'Hard to estimate. A lot to move, but it would have been a tiny job compared with the trench that was dug in the city between the Yamana and Hosokawa armies in the second year of the Onin War. Professor Kido said the surviving records claimed it was ten feet deep and twenty feet wide, and long enough to separate anything up to a hundred thousand or so soldiers on either side. I suppose he was particularly struck by it because of his own involvement in excavations. Imagine what treasures might be unearthed if that trench could be precisely located and excavated!'

Kimura smiled. 'It's probably underneath a whole block of multi-storey buildings. Buried for ever, I guess. While we were walking up from the taxi a while ago you said that Kido had seemed to be in good form the day you came here with him and Professor Yanagida, right?'

'I thought so, certainly. He was an enthusiast, and I got the impression that he was never happier than when looking at the physical remains of medieval Japan. Now that you mention it, though, he did seem to get rather upset for a while, just after telling me about the trench. He talked to Professor Yanagida in Japanese for a few minutes – they were both so generous in using English for my benefit most of the time, even to each other – and sounded almost angry about something. Then he turned to me and apologised, something about excavations being often troublesome, and changed the subject. I suppose it was something to do with his local authority advisory job in Kobe. Somebody told me he and his committee were supposed to be consulted every time a big building development project came up for approval, in case there might be a risk of disturbing important historical sites.'

*

'Well,' Philippa Kilpeck said when they eventually arrived back at the Sasayama bus terminal at a little before six. 'Thank you for a most interesting afternoon, Inspector.'

'And thank you. I learned a lot.' Kimura smiled. 'About the Onin War, and other things.'

'Are you returning to Kobe now?'

'Me? Oh, no. I have to meet my colleagues at Anraku-in for a discussion at six-thirty. And then I'm staying overnight here in Sasayama. I have a room booked at the Station Hotel, just across the street there. I, um . . . Dr Kilpeck?'

'Yes?'

'I don't suppose I could interest you in dining with me later this evening? On a purely social basis, I mean.'

'Do you know, Inspector, I believe you could. Purely socially, of course.'

Thirteen

William Ashley was among the first to arrive in the improvised lecturers' common room in the teaching block, and after a quick look round he glanced impatiently at his watch. Michiko Yanagida was already there talking quietly to Inger Lindblad. Old Miyamoto-sensei, the paper-maker, sat serenely in a corner by himself. By day and in his workshop he wore a short happi-coat over ordinary blue jeans, but of an evening he invariably appeared in a plain blue kimono which set off his wispy white beard admirably and gave him the look of a Chinese sage in an old ink painting.

The others began to arrive within a minute or two: Howard Bayliss in the company of Teramoto-sensei, the archery instructor, then Maggie Threlfall. These were closely followed by the Japanese language teacher Mr Kobayashi, attended by his three most devoted students, two short-haired young men from Singapore and the handsome and ferociously clever Reginald Kwok from Hong Kong. Somewhat to Ashley's surprise Professor Leclerc then appeared in the doorway, stood there leaning elegantly on his stick while he looked at leisure round the room, and then made his way to one of the two easy-chairs still unoccupied and settled himself in it.

Upwards of a dozen people in all had arrived by about ten past eight, when Ashley rapped a few times with his knuckles on the wooden arm of his chair and the murmur of general conversation died down. 'I guess we ought to get started. Friends, I want to thank you all for showing up this evening.

I called this special, informal meeting of the overseas members of the summer school and of instructors at pretty short notice, and I'm encouraged by your response. I propose that we should use English because the majority of us in this room are I think more comfortable in that language than in Japanese.' He looked a little uneasily in the direction of the linguistically touchy Professor Leclerc, but the Frenchman's face remained impassive. Encouraged, Ashley went on. 'And of course, all our expert instructors understand English.' He nodded courteously to Messrs Miyamoto and Teramoto, neither of whom had been heard to utter a word in English since the summer school had assembled.

'But naturally if any of our Japanese colleagues wishes to contribute to the discussion they are invited to do so in Japanese. We have interpreters enough among us to make sure that whatever they have to say will be understood by everybody. Is that okay?'

Nobody actually said yes, but there were indications of assent from here and there, and after a second or two Ashley went on. 'By now all of you know that the tragic death of our late academic director Professor Kido is the subject of a police investigation, led by Inspector Takeshi Hara from prefectural headquarters in Kobe. And many of us have already been interviewed by one or more police officers. May I just have a show of hands on that – how many of you have already been asked for statements?'

Raising his own hand, Ashley looked around. 'Thank you. A little more than half of us, it seems, plus probably about the same proportion of those who weren't able to make it to this meeting. I think we can assume that by the end of tomorrow the rest will have been seen. Now in case anybody assumes that as administrative director of the summer school I've been taken into the confidence of the police, let me make it clear that I have not. I don't have the smallest idea why the investigation was launched. Yes, Mr Weisse?'

It looked for a moment as if Manfred Weisse was about to

stand in order to address the gathering, but he merely sat bolt upright. 'It must surely be presumed that the authorities have learned of certain rumours which have been circulating since the death of Professor Kido.' In the deathly silence that followed his remark everybody scrupulously avoided looking at Maggie Threlfall, who herself looked perfectly composed.

Ashley hesitated before replying, and it was Howard Bayliss, the armour collector, who broke the silence. 'Speaking as an attorney, I'd say that the police in Japan would be no more inclined to commit a lot of expensive time and energy to an investigation on the basis of rumours alone than they would in America. As to the rumours, well, it's natural enough that people would speculate. We'd all seen Professor Kido seemingly healthy enough in the morning.'

'But he was at least fifty-five, perhaps nearly sixty, isn't it? Men of that age . . .' Inger Lindblad shrugged.

'A heart attack, I believe, ' Mr Kobayashi ventured. 'One of the Japanese students, pottery I think, mentioned that she had overheard one of the ambulance men say so. That is what I said to Inspector Hara when he interviewed me this afternoon.'

'Just a minute, just a minute, please.' Ashley raised a hand to still what looked like turning into a general argument. 'Please, let's forget about rumours for the moment. We aren't here this evening to launch a private enquiry of our own. All I intended to say to you all, and I repeat, is that as Mr Bayliss points out, the police must have some reason – other than rumour – for questioning us all. But that they haven't told me what it is. All I have to pass on to you from Inspector Hara is that they expect to be out of our hair at least by Monday or Tuesday next. And, of course, the school is due to end at noon Friday, with participants leaving Anraku-in during the afternoon. You have another question, Mr Weisse?'

'It is my first question. My earlier remarks were in the

nature of a hypothesis,' Weisse pointed out reprovingly. 'My question is this. If – I suppose following a post-mortem examination – the police have discovered evidence which suggests that there has been, what is the expression, a foul game—'

'Foul play, Manfred.'

'Thank you.' Weisse bowed slightly to Maggie Threlfall. 'Foul play, yes, of course. If foul play is now suspected *after* the death of Professor Kido, why then was there a police officer here at Anraku-in *before* he died?' He compressed his lips and glared at Ashley. 'And why, Mr Director, did you introduce him to a number of us as a journalist?'

*

'Ashley looked horribly embarrassed, as you may well imagine.' Michiko Yanagida smiled at the young woman sitting tidily on the one straight chair in her study-bedroom. She was herself perched on her bed, her legs drawn up girlishly to one side. It was a quarter to ten and the meeting had ended about twenty minutes earlier.

Michiko had been personally acquainted with Woman Senior Detective Junko Migishima for not much more than twenty-four hours, but she had taken to her at once and the more she saw of her the better she liked her. In fact even before Hara introduced them Michiko had heard quite a lot about Junko from her sister, and was predisposed in her favour. She didn't bother to remember all the bits and pieces of gossip that Hanae supplied with the tea whenever they met – usually at the house at Rokko when Otani was safely out of the way – but a good deal remained with her.

Specifically, Michiko knew that the Otanis had been guests at the reception following Junko's marriage to another police officer some years before, and that she had not only firmly resisted pressure to start a family, but also demonstrated her professional ability by securing promotion ahead of her husband. These last two items of information had stuck particularly in Michiko's mind because she strongly approved of such signs of female independence and initiative.

'He must have been. However did he answer? If he admitted that Inspector Kimura had fooled him he must have lost face tremendously.'

'He certainly would have done, but fortunately for him in that respect only, the German – he's a very accomplished calligrapher, by the way, I've seen some of his work – answered his own question. "I think we already know the explanation," he said in that rather cold voice of his. "It is because, of course, my hypothesis about the rumours is soundly based. They had been circulating for at least a week or so, and you and Kido had decided to invite the police to spy on us!" This caused a bit of an uproar, he began to shout and I didn't quite understand everything he said after that. Something about reporting Ashley to the German Embassy, I think, and maybe suing the Anraku-in board of management.'

'I see. So what happened then?' Junko's normally cheerful urchin face looked quite solemn.

'The Australian woman, Threlfall, started shouting too, something to the effect that it hadn't done much good, had it, and that she hoped the other police – that's you and Inspector Hara and the others, of course – would do a better job of investigating the murder than Inspector Kimura had done in preventing it.' Michiko blushed. 'In fact she referred to Mr Kimura by an obscene name.'

'You should hear some of the things we call him behind his back at headquarters,' Junko said calmly. 'Well, thank you very much for putting me in the picture, sensei. I'm assuming the meeting broke up after that?'

'Yes. The American, Howard Bayliss, is very level-headed and tried to calm people down but it was hopeless.' Michiko lowered her voice. 'In fact,' she murmured with a meaning look at the party wall of the room, 'my Danish neighbour Ms Lindblad seemed to be thoroughly enjoying the row. The Japanese, I need hardly say, behaved themselves perfectly. Teramoto-sensei's a Zen priest, of course, so you'd expect him to be calm, and Miyamoto- sensei just smiled, as though he were watching a lot of squabbling children. I quite like foreigners myself, but they really are peculiar, aren't they? Take Ashley, for instance. I can't imagine why he called the meeting in the first place. After all, the only thing he actually told us was that he had nothing to tell us.'

Junko smiled. 'Gaijin certainly have their funny little ways. I've been talking to Shoko Yasuda this evening. This is nothing to do with the case, but she mentioned that as many as three of them have tried to get her into bed since the summer school began. Not all at the same time, I hasten to add, and I'd better not mention any names.'

Michiko raised her eyes to the ceiling. '*Men!*' she said, with bitter contempt, and Junko grinned even more widely.

'Well, two of them were, at least,' she said, with a quick, wicked glance at the wall.

*

After leaving Michiko Yanagida's room, Junko paid a visit to the women's washroom in the same corridor, and was washing her hands when she heard the flop of plastic slippers passing the door. It sounded like more than one pair, and she thought she might have just caught the murmur of voices, but wasn't sure. Anyway, the wearer or wearers of the slippers had come from the direction of the entrance to the building. Hurriedly turning off the water, she stood very still and definitely heard the sound of a nearby door being first opened and then a few seconds later closed again.

Junko was curious. She opened the washroom door, satisfied herself that the corridor was now deserted, took off her own slippers and moved barefoot and silently in the direction from which the sound of the door had come. There were only three in that stretch of the corridor and Junko was pretty sure that the first of them was the one she was interested in.

She looked at the card in the holder. 'DR PHILIPPA KILPECK'. And yes, it was Dr Kilpeck who was entertaining. Junko's knowledge of spoken English was to all intents and purposes non-existent, but needless to say she recognised it, and had no doubt that it wasn't a radio she could hear. For though the woman's voice wasn't familiar to her, the man's most certainly was. And Inspector Kimura, also widely and pejoratively known among his subordinates as Gorgeous, Pretty Boy and The Menace, wouldn't be at all pleased if he were to discover her tip-toeing about outside the room.

On the other hand they'd only just gone in. Surely it would be safe enough to stay for at least half a minute and get a better impression of the tone of the conversation – it sounded friendly enough and that was an undoubtedly amused chuckle although abruptly cut off – so as to . . . Junko's hand flew to her mouth to stifle a gasp and her heart pounded as the handle of the door a few inches in front of her moved fractionally. Then she gradually relaxed, and the smile never far away from her mobile mouth took possession.

Nobody was about to leave the room. Certainly not for a while, anyway, because unless she was very much mistaken, that short burst of feminine laughter had been stopped by a kiss, and either Gorgeous or the cool blonde from England herself had just locked the door from inside.

Fourteen

'Yes, well, perhaps that would be best, if you're sure you don't mind. I'm finding more to occupy me here than I expected, but we'll definitely reckon to get away by about three, say. Before you two go off together, though,' Otani said, 'I'd like you to show me where the archery class meets, Michiko. If you know, that is.'

'I do, yes. It's at the other side of the teaching block. Over there.' Leaving the residential block in which the late Professor Kido had met his end, Otani had seen Hanae and Michiko strolling towards the Anraku-in headquarters building, and with a murmured apology to Hara cut across to intercept them.

It had been at his suggestion that Hanae had joined him in the official car for the one and a half-hour drive from their house to Sasayama. It was Sunday, after all, he pointed out, and he didn't see why he should be deprived of her company for the whole day. The only reason he was going at all was to look around the place, and have a few words with Kimura and the others. Perhaps one or two of the Japanese participants as well. Shouldn't take long, and Hanae would be happy enough to chat with Michiko for an hour or so if necessary, wouldn't she?

As soon as they were within range, Otani had made contact with the officer manning the radio telephone in the Sasayama police car stationed at Anraku-in and told him their estimated time of arrival; but even so had been a little surprised when his devoted driver Tomita drew up with a flourish at the main entrance to see both Hara and Michiko waiting to greet them, and breaking off what looked like an enjoyably animated conversation to do so.

A busy hour and a half had passed since then, mostly in conversations with Hara, with Kimura, and with the secretary Shoko Yasuda in the presence of Woman Senior Detective Migishima. Otani had too many ideas surging round in his head to notice that Hanae had a look in her eye that meant she'd heard something particularly fascinating, but at any rate she was obviously in no hurry at all to go home, and quite content to go with Michiko to find some lunch.

Michiko led them past the bicycle racks at the entrance to the teaching block and on to the far side of the two-storey building, which was separated from what appeared to be a boundary wall by a strip of land some three metres wide. The wall itself was about two metres high and made of untreated concrete breeze-blocks – dreary enough in itself but rendered particularly forbidding, almost sinister, by the fact that it was topped with barbed wire.

'Not much of an outlook from the downstairs windows,' Otani commented. 'If you ask me, it looks like a prison camp from here. I'm surprised they left all this empty space. People generally cram buildings as close to boundary walls as they can. As indeed they have done, at the far end there.'

'Well, there's no mystery about that at least,' Michiko said. 'I'm told that this piece of land was always intended to be used as an archery range. There are plans to turn it into a proper enclosure eventually.'

Hanae shivered slightly. 'Well, it certainly isn't very cheerful as it is.'

'I agree. Thank you, Michiko. Why don't you two leave me to it now? Enjoy your lunch, and I'll see you both later.'

Left to himself and having momentarily forgotten about Hara, Otani paced the length of strip of ground, and estimated it at about thirty metres. Long enough, if on the narrow side, for a practice range, and as a matter of fact a sensible, safe place to put one. There was no door on that side of the building, and few windows on the ground floor. Those were situated towards the near end of the range, so that even the most inept archer aiming at the target couldn't possibly break one by accident, much less endanger anybody inside one of the rooms.

Otani scuffed at the ground with the heel of his right shoe. It was hard, but appeared to be of compounded earth, carefully levelled and, it seemed, regularly swept. When, still at the far end, he looked more closely at it, he thought he could see the marks left by the easel-like target supports, and wondered where they and the other equipment were stored when not in use.

The teaching block occupied a corner of the Anraku-in site and its far end was much closer to its neighbouring wall than the side, a matter of a foot away at most. It might just be possible for a person to squeeze through the space between them, but whoever had planned the archery range had obviously thought about that. At the end of the building a box-like housing contained a high, stout wooden panel which, Otani discovered when he made the experiment, slid out smoothly on runners and could be locked into place hard against the wall. When the range was in use, the dangerous end could be sealed off completely.

'It is as well to guard against the possibility that a small child, or animal perhaps, might stray unwittingly into danger.'

The sentiment was unexceptionable, the voice calm, and Otani nearly jumped out of his skin, because the speaker was standing just behind him and his approach had been soundless. With a great effort of will he forced himself to remain motionless for a second and then turned slowly to face the stranger.

He was a man who was, Otani guessed, of about the same age as himself, but he gave the impression of inhabiting a time dimension of his own, linked only tenuously with the one the generality of people tried to adjust to. In spite of the heat he was wearing a plain blue woollen kimono, and the skin of his face and neck was the colour of old ivory; smooth and dry but somehow translucent, as though there were fewer than the usual number of layers to it. He was almost bald, with just a frothy horseshoe of white hair at the back of his scalp terminating above each ear, but he had a thin, wispy white beard that sprouted from the centre of his chin only.

Otani bowed, but not very low, and noticed as he did so that the man was wearing flat *zori* on his otherwise bare feet. The stranger's bow of acknowledgment was a little deeper, and when he spoke again it was to apologise.

'I fear that I have intruded upon your privacy, sir.'

'Not at all. I am the intruder here, I think. My name is Otani, and I am a police officer. Have I the honour of speaking to Teramoto-sensei, the master archer?'

'You flatter me, sir. Teramoto is a man of refinement, a priest and a man in whose veins flows noble blood. Our names are not dissimilar, but I am a mere artisan.' He bowed again. 'Miyamoto. Paper-maker. Please show your favour towards me.'

In principle, there was nothing Otani liked better than swapping elaborate old-fashioned courtesies with men of culture. On the other hand it was getting on for twelve noon, and standing about in a bleak cul-de-sac at the back of a shabby classroom block wasn't conducive to phrase-making.

'I'm pleased to make your acquaintance, sensei,' he said briskly. 'I understand this area is to be fitted out as a proper, permanent archery range in due course.'

'I believe it is.'

'My colleague Inspector Hara tells me that you have already been good enough to give him a statement in connection with our investigation into the circumstances of the death of the late Professor Kido.'

'I have, yes. Not that he could have found my answers to his questions to be of much interest.'

Otani treated him to his coldest stare. 'It had occurred to me that you might have approached me here because you had remembered something you omitted to mention to the inspector.'

Miyamoto returned the stare calmly. 'No. You were pointed out to me from a distance, Superintendent, and when I saw you come here with Professor Yanagida and the other lady and then remain after they left, I decided to follow and see what manner of man you are.'

'I see. Well, that's your privilege, I suppose. Let me ask you something, sensei. Your home is in Kyushu, isn't it?'

'It is.'

'A very long way away from here.'

'At one time it was. Now the journey takes a mere two hours by All Nippon Airways, plus another hour or so at each end of the flight.'

'Very true. You are outspoken, sensei and that's reputed to be a characteristic of Kyushu people. Did your family originally hail from there?'

'No, they did not. Osaka people are also said to be forthright. I lost my accent many years ago, but I was born not so far away from here.'

'Were you acquainted with Professor Kido before you joined the staff of this summer school?'

'Certainly. Kido and I knew each other as boys, and kept in sporadic touch over the years.'

'Indeed? Did you tell Inspector Hara this?'

'No sir, I did not.'

'Why not?'

'Because he didn't ask, but you did. On the other hand he did ask me to give an account of my movements between the time Kido was seen to go to his room on the day of his death and the time Miss Yasuda raised the alarm, and you have not. I answer the questions of duly authorised officials straightforwardly, Superintendent, but I see no reason to volunteer information, whether about my boyhood or anything else.'

'All right, I suppose I can't complain about that, unless you are withholding information which you might reasonably suppose to be relevant to this particular investigation. If you are, it is your duty as a citizen to divulge it.'

'Superintendent, let me remind you that the people currently assembled in this place are for the most part educated, intelligent adults. Yet so far as I know, none of us has been told precisely what it is you are investigating. We infer that the police have reason to suspect that Kido was murdered. Are we right? Until we know the answer to that question, how can we possibly judge what may or may not be relevant to your enquiries?'

'Miyamoto-sensei, I accept that you and your colleagues must have made certain assumptions. But police officers are not at liberty to use words like "murder" except in the strict legal sense. It must be obvious that we aren't satisfied that Professor Kido's death was due to natural causes – ah, there you are, Inspector! I'm so sorry I deserted you like that, but I've been having a fascinating conversation with Miyamoto-sensei. He tells me that he never objects to giving straight answers to questions put to him by authorised officials. So here's one last question for you before I must tear myself away, sensei. Did you like Professor Kido?'

Miyamoto fondled his sparse beard, taking his time over replying, and when he did speak it was in a considered way. 'Kido was not wholly dislikable. He retained a certain engaging quality of enthusiasm. He was, I'm given to understand, a gifted teacher, generous to students and junior colleagues, but pompous in public, and excessively sensitive about his professional reputation. He was vain about his various public appointments, and was rather obviously hoping to receive some sort of honour eventually. The Order of the Chrysanthemum, perhaps. He enjoyed exercising his bureaucratic powers, and delighted in being obstructive when handling planning applications. On balance, no, I did not like him, and nor I suspect did a lot of other people.'

*

'Hara, I'm very much afraid that I'm going to find myself apologising to Kimura before long.'

'What about, sir?'

'Well, remember it was Kimura who pointed out the coincidence. The nark who was shot in Osaka was called Miyamoto. He was trying to sell Ninja information about Hosoda, and there isn't much doubt that he was shot in order to shut his mouth. We know that Hosoda has – or had, if he's dead – links with Takeuchi's syndicate, as does this mystery man Zenji Ono, the president of a major property development company. And now we have *this* Miyamoto, who looks like somebody in a Chinese ink painting but is a very cool customer indeed who turns out to have been born and brought up in this area. He blandly reminds us that the late Kido, as archaeological adviser to the prefectural government, was inclined to enjoy making difficulties over planning applications. To think there might be a connection between the two Miyamotos doesn't look anything like as ridiculous as it did.'

Hara looked startled. 'Miyamoto born near here?'

'Osaka or somewhere close to there.'

'May I ask how you know, sir?'

'I asked him. All right, now listen. I know this is a pretty shaky hypothesis at present, and apart from the name it's hard to imagine much in common between a garbage man and petty crook on the one hand and a famous craftsman on the other. He *is* famous, is he?'

'Very famous. He's been officially designated by the government as an intangible cultural asset. His hand-made Japanese paper is about the most expensive that artists and calligraphers can buy.'

'Nevertheless he referred to himself as an artisan, and of course that's technically what he is. I mean, paper-making isn't a profession demanding academic qualifications, just a very long apprenticeship, natural flair and years of experience working under a master. A boy coming from a very humble background could, eventually, quite possibly become a leading craftsman and be respected as such, right?'

'Well, yes . . .'

'And you know what role-players we Japanese are, Hara. If a person's treated as an eminent cultural figure that's the image he or she's going to cultivate. I can't make up my mind whether I like Miyamoto or not, but he's unquestionably an accomplished actor.'

'Do you seriously think he might have murdered Kido, sir?'

'Put it like this. I think he might conceivably have a motive, which extraordinarily enough could be linked with Hosoda and the Osaka shooting. And there's something else . . . no, that wants a lot more thinking about before I try it out on you. For the moment, I want you to put somebody to work on tracing this Miyamoto's origins. We need to know whether he is related, however distantly, to the Osaka Miyamoto. And a simultaneous check on that one's antecedents, needless to say. Secondly, get somebody discreet to look up the record of major planning applications received by the prefectural government during the past few years and on which Kido and his advisory committee had anything to say. Specifically, of course, to keep a sharp eye out for any objections Kido may have made in connection with applications lodged by Ono's company – what's it called?'

'Elite Property Developments.'

'Right. And finally, I want on my desk first thing in the morning an inventory of the items that bright young woman Yasuda took out of Kido's room. They were sent to the regional forensic lab. They can carry on working on them; all I want's the list.'

*

'Well, let's have it,' Otani said as soon as Tomita had driven away. He unlocked the sliding outer gate of their house and stood back to let Hanae through. 'You've obviously been bursting to tell me something all the way home. Even Tomita realised it, I think. His ears were swivelling about like radar dishes, and all you talked about was the grilled eel you had for lunch.'

'You're quite right, as usual, but I'm not sure you're going to like this. Michiko seems to have fallen for Inspector Hara.'

Fifteen

Tomita the driver duly turned up at Rokko as instructed, half an hour earlier than usual, and was surprised when Otani said that he wanted to go to headquarters by way of the prefectural library. Tomita pointed out that the library didn't open until ten, and that come to think of it he had a feeling that it might be closed all day on Mondays; but the Chief didn't seem to be listening, so with a mental shrug he did what he was told.

Otani had heard what Tomita said, but was unconcerned. If the day ever came when his personal and official authority proved to be insufficient to get him through the staff entrance to a public building anywhere in the prefecture, it would be time to think about shaving his head and becoming a priest. Besides, he had many more important and interesting things to think about.

What Hanae had told him about Michiko and Hara definitely fell into the latter category, but one could hope that it wouldn't also find a place in the former. Otani had never given much thought to Michiko's private affairs, vaguely assuming that she was so wrapped up in her university teaching career and the various campaigns she supported and organisations she belonged to that she had no time for personal relationships. Apart, that is, from her close sisterly bond with Hanae. Years ago Michiko had, he recalled, been keen on a scientist of some kind. A physicist, that was it, but whether the relationship had ever amounted to a love affair even Hanae professed not to know.

Apparently, however, Michiko told Hanae that she'd experienced something of a *coup de foudre* on meeting Hara in the coffee shop near Anraku-in, and that she found him disturbingly attractive. While Hara in his turn had more or less admitted having been fairly bowled over by Michiko. Wonders would never cease.

In every respect but two they might well suit each other splendidly. Though not a scholar, Hara was a very well educated man with intellectual tastes, as erudite in his way as Michiko. His stately courtesy and, for a Japanese, advanced views on the rights of women would go down well with her; and while he could not by any stretch of the imagination be described as a good-looking man, Hara was at least tall and well covered.

Hara was also, alas, ten years younger than Michiko, and married with two small children. According to Hanae, Michiko had worked out his age very early on by asking him about his studies at Nagasaki University, and was neither embarrassed nor defensive about it. Why, she had quite reasonably argued, was it thought quite in order for a man to have an affair with a woman ten years his junior, but stigmatised as cradle-snatching when it happened the other way round? As for his being married, Michiko had announced that she wanted Hara as a friend and lover, not a husband, and had no intention of imperilling his marriage. They had already discussed this, she claimed.

The extraordinary thing was that, originating in a fortuitous meeting and an awareness of a mutual attraction, things seemed to have moved so far so fast. That the inhibited Hara and the touchy, feminist Michiko should within a couple of days of their first encounter have progressed to chatting to each other about the logistics of embarking on a clandestine love affair was nothing short of astounding.

Otani heaved a sigh as the prefectural library came into view and Tomita began to fuss again. 'Just go round to the side,' he said curtly. 'Find the staff or goods entrance or whatever, let me off there and go and get yourself a cup of coffee or something. This could take me up to an hour, but I'll try to make it less.'

Clearly fearing the worst, Tomita piloted the Toyota Police Special round the building at a snail's pace. As Otani had expected, there was a goods entrance at the back. Moreover, the doors were open and a janitor wearing a warehouseman's protective brown coat was watching the driver of a Nittsu Express delivery van stacking packages on to a wheeled trolley. Both men looked up, startled to see a police car pulling up.

Otani smiled to himself when Tomita leapt out of the car, went over to the janitor and evidently set about impressing on him the status and distinction of the visitor he had brought. Clambering out himself, he decided it was time to forget about Hara and Michiko for a while. Police officers had been known to go in for love affairs before now, and in the nature of things a good many of them quite likely involved close relatives of other police officers. Michiko was hardly an unprincipled femme fatale, and whatever his private preoccupations, Hara still seemed to be capable of leading a murder investigation reasonably efficiently. They must sort out their own lives.

The immediate task in hand was to find out whether he had indeed worked out how Kido had been murdered.

*

'You see, Ninja,' he said to Noguchi a couple of hours later, 'it struck me that if the two incidents my wife's sister had witnessed were in fact serious attempts to kill Kido, or even just terrify him, the methods used were what you might call old-fashioned, and employed in classical Japanese settings. The collapse of a subsidiary shrine building practically on top of Kido's head at the Hiyoshi Taisha. A traditional Japanese arrow shot through a window. The sort of tricks

131

your namesakes the *ninja* could easily have got up to in the old days.'

'So?'

'So when I met this quick-witted Miyamoto fellow and considered him as a suspect – mainly because of the name and the Osaka connection, I admit – I thought him the sort of man who could easily have amused himself by staging episodes of that kind before finally polishing Kido off with a more subtle ploy of the same general nature. Miyamoto's a conceited man, and he gets himself up in traditional clothes, has a beard and so forth. It was his antique appearance that set me thinking on those lines.'

'Think he might have used some sort of judo hold on Kido? Can't see that myself. Pathologist would have noticed bruising near the carotid artery.'

'No, not that. Remember this man's a leading expert on Japanese hand-made paper, *washi*. My old father was a bit of a calligrapher, and I remember watching him for hours on end when I was a boy. He once took me with him to the shop where he used to buy his paper. I was astounded to find out how much it cost, and it stuck in my mind that he said it was expensive because you could do all sorts of things with it as well as use it to write poems and letters on, including getting rid of people you didn't like.'

'What was that supposed to mean?'

'I didn't have the slightest idea at the time, but I spent an hour browsing through books about washi this morning, and I think I understand what he was hinting at now. Classical murder methods in Japan were for the most part as obvious in their way as they are today, because there was seldom any need to try to conceal the fact that the victim *had* been murdered. But when some sort of political or family intrigue, or perhaps an inheritance was involved, the killer might need to make the death appear to have been natural. Well, poisoning was one obvious method, a lot easier to get away with in the old days than now I suppose.

But it seems that handmade paper was a favourite murder weapon in such cases, and I think Miyamoto used it on Kido.'

'Well, come on. How?'

'According to the books, all the killer has to do is watch the victim in his sleep for a minute or two, then place a wet piece of washi over his nose and mouth immediately after he's breathed out. The paper clings and completely blocks the airways, making it impossible to inhale. Naturally the victim's going to wake up and struggle but it's only necessary for the murderer to lie on top of him and pin his arms down for ten or twenty seconds before he suffocates. Another minute to make quite sure, then peel the paper off and there you are – a suffocated corpse with no marks on the face.'

'Neat.'

'Very. And we know that Kido might have caught a chill, was almost certainly feeling groggy anyway because he'd taken a couple of codeine tablets. Wouldn't have been able to put up much of a struggle.'

'Going to have a job proving it.'

'True enough. Not one of that lot up there at Anraku-in has got anything like a watertight alibi for the residential buildings. People were coming and going all through the lunch hour and during the free time afterwards. It so happens that Miyamoto's own room is in the same block as Kido's was, so nobody who saw him there would have paid any attention to him. A minor point in itself, of course, but when he and I have our next little chat he's going to have to keep his wits about him. With a bit of luck he'll fall to pieces once he realises we're on to the method.'

Noguchi shook his head. The movement amounted to no more than a centimetre or so each way, but conveyed a powerful impression of scepticism. 'Dodgy, if you ask me. District prosecutor'll fall about laughing if you try it on him.'

'Possibly, but let me try this on you.' Otani got up and

went over to his desk, returning with a sheet of paper in his hand. 'You remember we were told the secretary thought there was something funny going on. So the moment Kido's body had been taken to the ambulance she cleared his room and stowed everything away, right? Well, this is a copy of the inventory. It includes an item described as "contents of waste-paper basket, contained in plastic bag". I got on to the phone when I saw that, and forensic confirmed to me that there were only three things in that bag, One was a copy of the previous day's *Kobe Shimbun*, obviously disposed of after having been read. The second was an empty cigarette packet, Mild Seven brand. And the third was a piece of high-quality hand-made Japanese paper, which we may assume had been damp, because there were beads of condensation on the inner surface of the plastic bag the girl put it in and sealed with one of those wire twists.'

*

'You don't *have* to stay at the Kyoto Ladies' Hotel after you leave here at the end of the week, you know,' Kimura said wistfully, his hands resting lightly on Philippa Kilpeck's slender shoulders. 'There's plenty of room in my apartment. I mean, you say you definitely have to go back to England early next month, but until then . . .'

'Before then, I have work to do,' she said sternly, and then kissed him on one cheek. 'And besides, I'm not in the habit of moving in even temporarily with gentlemen I've only recently met. However attractive they may be. I can assure you that I'm counting on seeing you again before I have to leave Japan. Thank you for showing me the hotel in the first place, and for ringing up and booking a room for me. I'm sorry you and Inspector Hara have to go back to Kobe today.'

'Oh, it's only to pull together some paper work and tie up loose ends. I expect we'll be back here at Anraku-in again before the end of the week.'

'To arrest the murderer, you mean?'

'I probably shouldn't be saying this to you, but quite possibly, yes. Mrs Migishima will be staying on until everything's sorted out, and an officer from Sasayama police station will be on duty too. If you want to get in touch with me you have only to get Shoko Yasuda to say to either of them. What's wrong, Philippa? You've gone very pale.'

She clung to him and rested her face against his shoulder for a moment. When she looked up again there were tears in her eyes. 'I'm sorry. And I'm ashamed. Of allowing myself to enjoy your company so much that I forget for hours on end why you're here. Poor, poor Professor Kido. Jiro, did somebody here really kill him?'

'There's not much doubt about that.'

'And you know who it was?'

'Not personally, no. Not yet. And obviously I couldn't tell you even if I did. We've all been busy in our different ways, and Hara's had people working on related things in Kobe. He and I will be talking things through with our boss this afternoon. You didn't meet Superintendent Otani yesterday, did you?'

'No. Michiko Yanagida pointed him out to me. He looked very forbidding. Strange to think he's her brother-in-law.'

'He might look forbidding, but he's a very smart man. Even smarter than me, Philippa. If he's figured out how Kido was killed I'll take his word for it. And if he says he knows who did it, then yes, we will be coming back pretty soon to pick the murderer up.'

*

'So to sum up, gentlemen,' Otani concluded, 'there is to my mind no doubt that Miyamoto killed Kido, and by the method I have described. I believe that we shall find in due course that his reasons for doing so arise from his connections – my apologies for pooh-pooing the idea when you first mentioned it, Kimura-kun – with the missing Keizo Hosoda, the Takeuchi crime syndicate, Zenji Ono's property development company, and the shooting of the other Miyamoto, the Osaka informer.'

'And presumably you don't want to pull Miyamoto in before we've put some arrangements in place for handling the yakuza end.'

'Precisely. Ninja has been able to confirm through his sources that the man who was shot was indeed a low-grade errand runner for the Takeuchi syndicate. In a position not only to pick up bits and pieces of confidential information and very rashly try to sell them, but also of course to serve as a channel of communication to the other Miyamoto. Whose family tree it seems to be taking your people a long time to trace, Hara.'

'My apologies, sir. There have been distractions—'

Otani cut him off coldly. 'So I understand, but let that pass. I am surer than ever that the two men will turn out to have been kinsmen of some kind. I hope you'll be able to confirm that during the course of tomorrow. In the morning I have an appointment with the head of the planning department of the prefectural government, and after that I propose to go and have a chat with Mr Zenji Ono.'

Sixteen

'Migishima-san! Excuse me, but could I have a private word with you?'

Junko stopped, turned and saw Michiko Yanagida almost at her elbow, slightly out of breath from having hurried to intercept her. 'Yes of course, sensei.'

'I was just coming out of the dormitory block and saw you. I expect you're busy, but if you could spare ten minutes or so?' Michiko looked around the open space. There were a few other people about, but nobody within earshot. 'I, er, I'm sorry to be mysterious, but is there anywhere we could go where we can't be overheard?'

Junko pondered, studying the face of the woman she still found great difficulty in thinking of as the commander's sister-in-law. She was far from being easily awed, but Superintendent Otani's reputation at headquarters was such that it came as something of a surprise to realise that he had relatives like ordinary people. Professor Yanagida looked worried, and would have to be humoured.

'I have a key to the private reception room attached to the main auditorium. It's off limits to summer school members but the police have access to it for private conferences. We'll go there, shall we?'

As the two women made their way to Anraku-in's impressive main entrance Junko hoped very much that she wasn't about to be treated to any embarrassing personal confidences. Her job description said nothing about acting as personal assistant to Inspector Hara as head of the criminal-investigation section, but since her promotion she had found herself working closely with him, and liking him more and more as she got to know him well. At first amused to notice – as she did almost at once – that Hara had taken a fancy to the high-powered woman professor, Junko was beginning to feel uneasy about the situation. Especially as Michiko had let drop a number of highly complimentary remarks about him in the course of their chats. What with Gorgeous Kimura pretty obviously having something going with the English woman and now Hara and this one eyeing each other, the atmosphere at the summer school was beginning to warm up to an alarming degree.

The lobby was as usual deserted, and so was the side corridor serving the offices behind it. Junko took a ring with a yellow plastic tab attached to it from her shoulder bag, and used one of the keys on it to switch the small elevator on. The doors opened at once, and she ushered Michiko in. The control buttons inside offered the simple choice between 'UP' and 'DOWN'.

'This is normally only used by the head of the religious sect and VIP guests,' Junko explained as the lift slid smoothly upwards. It stopped and the doors opened to reveal a spacious, luxuriously furnished reception room. Its deep burgundy carpet must have been specially designed, since it featured a lurid golden sunburst in the centre, the design repeated in three dimensional form in an ornate chandelier suspended immediately above it. A large framed monochrome photograph of an elderly lady in an old-fashioned kimono had pride of place on one wall, above an altar-like side table on which stood a fine flower arrangement. There was an ordinary walnut-veneered door in each side wall, while the one opposite the lift was dominated by a pair of lofty double doors.

'I'm told this room's crammed with flowers when the Founder's Representative comes here. Her grandson, actually, but that's what they call him.'

138

'He doesn't live here, then?'

'No. The sect's actually run from Tokyo where the offices are. He has a penthouse apartment above what they call the branch temple there. We've been asked not to go into either of the side rooms, but it's very comfortable here and we won't be disturbed. Let's sit down, shall we?' Having re-locked the lift, Junko settled herself in one of several expensive-looking armchairs and after a moment's hesitation Michiko took a similar one at her side. 'Well, what can I do for you?'

'I find myself in a curious position,' Michiko began, and Junko's heart sank. 'Because – I'm not sure if Inspector Hara has told you this – well, in a way, I was the one who started all this.' Oh dear, worse and worse: the throaty way she said the name Hara, the onset of a confession for sure. 'You see, I was with Professor Kido when he was nearly killed at the Hiyoshi Taisha, and again when the arrow flew into the common room and just missed him. And I told my sister's husband, and' – she made a gesture of hopelessness with open hands, palms raised – 'well, that's why you're here now, I suppose.'

Having braced herself to show suitable solidarity with another woman in an emotional predicament, while at the same time firmly resolved not to allow herself to be drawn into a heart-to-heart, Junko was slow to grasp the idea that Michiko seemed to be heading in a different direction. She became confused, lost the thread and picked up her remarks again some seconds later.

'. . . realise of course that this doesn't in any way entitle me to any privileges. Indeed, since Inspector Hara is clearly the soul of discretion, so far as his official work is concerned, for all I know I may be a suspect myself.'

'I may be talking out of turn, but I think I can safely reassure you on that point,' Junko said, having sorted out her thoughts. 'Inspector Hara told me he can't remember a witness ever dictating such a cogent and helpful statement before,' she added, deciding that a little sisterly encouragement wouldn't come amiss after all.

'Did he really?'

'Oh yes.'

'How very flattering.' The room was cool to the point of chilliness, but Michiko's cheeks were pink. 'But that is by the way. The reason I asked to speak to you was because I thought it my duty to report that the relations between at least some of the members of the summer school have become extremely strained, especially during the last day or so.'

'I've been getting that impression myself, even though I'm an outsider. Do go on.'

'I suppose that after all the flurry of interviewing over the weekend people were rather expecting some quick resolution. That is, of a dramatic nature, such as an arrest. Rather than this sort of suspended animation. People are going through the motions of studying and carrying on with their various activities, but it is awfully difficult to concentrate. I don't want to retail gossip for the sake of it, but I am quite concerned about some individuals.'

'May I ask who, in particular?'

'Of course. I told you about Manfred Weisse's outburst at the special meeting Bill Ashley called. Well, he's still going about complaining about being spied on, and snapping at Ashley. Maggie Threlfall isn't helping things in the least. Maybe it's her idea of a joke, but every time she comes into the common room she makes some loud, tasteless remark, speculating about the identity of the murderer. Even Professor Leclerc's started making sour remarks about Inspector Hara. Referring to him as Inspector Maigret and suggesting he might make better progress if he tried smoking a pipe.'

Junko smiled, and immediately apologised for doing so. 'It's just that I don't think a pipe would suit him at all. I'm not treating what you say lightly, needless to say. This must obviously be very distressing for everybody. All the same, I'm afraid it can't be helped.'

'I suppose not, but that's not all. I really believe that Bill Ashley's close to a breakdown, and poor Miss Yasuda's bearing the brunt of it. He seems to have become obsessed with the idea that it's all her fault.'

'Her fault? In what way?'

'Well, he keeps implying none too subtly that it was Miss Yasuda who first persuaded you – the police I mean – to even consider that Professor Kido might have been murdered. That in fact he probably did die from natural causes and nobody would have thought anything else for a second if it hadn't been for her—'

'I'm sorry to interrupt, but listen, sensei. There's a lot I don't yet know about this case, and I'm not at liberty to tell you much of what I do know, but unofficially and in confidence, let me make a few things very plain to you. First, there is no doubt whatever that Professor Kido was murdered. I don't myself know how it was done, but I believe my superiors do. I also believe that before long they will know who did it, and will then easily work out why. And when the time comes, Shoko Yasuda's testimony will be absolutely vital—' Junko stopped abruptly and turned to look at the tall double doors behind Michiko. 'What was that?'

Michiko looked bewildered. 'What was what?'

Shaking her head in irritation and with a finger to her mouth, Junko rose with one swift movement, crossed to the double doors and listened for a moment. Then she grabbed the handle of the right-hand door, twisted and wrenched at it. It was locked, and with a muttered curse Junko fumbled with the key-ring she had been holding throughout their conversation, found the right key and unlocked it. No more than two or three seconds had elapsed since she first touched the handle, but it was too long. By the time she was through the door and had negotiated the heavy curtain beyond, whoever had been on the other side had reached one of the main doors at the back of the darkened auditorium and slipped out. Both women heard the swish and hiss of the door closing.

Junko and Michiko stared at each other. Suddenly it was the formerly poised, businesslike policewoman who looked young and vulnerable, and the previously worried academic who exuded calm authority. 'You'd better get on the phone and report this to Inspector Hara,' Michiko said. 'While I go and look for Miss Yasuda.'

*

Shoko Yasuda looked up from her desk, and smiled with relief when she saw who her visitor was. All the unhappiness, stress and anxiety of the past few days seemed to have wrought havoc with her command of spoken English, normally quite good. Bill Ashley only spoke to her in Japanese when he was in a good mood, which was never since the death of Professor Kido. The Japanese staff and students never seemed to need her help, but most of the gaijin who communicated in English and tended to haunt her office were as edgy and disagreeable as Ashley, and made her tongue-tied. So it was a pleasant change to be able to use her own language.

'I'm sorry to disturb you when you're busy.'

'Oh, that's perfectly all right.'

'Is Ashley-san in his office at the moment?'

'No, I'm afraid he won't be back here before lunch-time. Is there anything I can do?'

'No. You've done more than enough as it is.'

*

Otani emerged from the offices of the prefectural town planning department considerably better informed in various respects, but not much the wiser in others. The visit had started badly, with Otani being received not by the director but on his behalf by a depressing functionary who sheepishly mumbled something to the effect that the top man had been summoned urgently to a conference.

Otani was much too wise in the ways of bureaucrats to believe that for a moment, but listened all the same with ostentatious politeness to the wretched substitute's tedious explanation of the checks and safeguards built into the department's approval procedures. These, Otani was assured several times, were such that it was inconceivable that any improper pressure whether of a political or a financial nature could ever be brought to bear at any stage in the handling of a planning application, much less that any such pressure could influence the outcome. The interview was a total waste of Otani's time, and at the end of ten minutes of his mendacious nonsense the dim official handed him over with manifest relief to an altogether different sort of man.

This was the secretary to the archaeological advisory panel, a Mr Araki, who bore Otani off to his own cubbyhole of an office. Araki looked like a cartoonist's idea of a mad scientist, being egg-bald on top but with bushy thickets of hair sticking wildly and horizontally out of his skull above each enormous ear. There could be no doubt as to the sincerity of his grief over the death of Professor Kido, his panel's chairman; but enthusiasm kept breaking through. The man clearly loved his job, and the top of his desk was soon littered with half-unrolled maps, plans and drawings.

At the end of half an hour Otani knew, and thought he would very likely remember, that the area round the city of Kobe, now incorporating the historic port of Hyogo, had been fought over for centuries, and that the traces of numerous battles between contending warlords lay not far below the surface in all sorts of places. That the old port had been a centre for trade with the Asian mainland, particularly between the eighth and twelfth centuries, and of the tally trade with the Chinese Ming dynasty of the fifteenth and sixteenth.

In Araki's splendidly eccentric opinion, no new building should be permitted in the Kobe area at all, and all the existing ones should be torn down to permit a *systematic* programme of excavation. Who could possibly know what treasures lay below the streets of late twentieth-century Kobe?

Professor Kido inclined to put obstacles in the way of developers? But of course, my dear sir, and quite right too! After all, his own distinguished academic reputation had been built on his discovery of the extraordinary Kitano Buddha, the hollow wooden image inside which he and a gaijin research assistant had found a scroll dating it very precisely as having been written in the mid twelfth century. And, having come across references to a family temple said to have been founded in the same period on the very edge of the site of the appalling so-called Royal Heights development—the very one the gentleman is interested in, yes indeed, the professor had entertained some hope of other remarkable finds. To have excavated the small area affected – here, you can see it clearly indicated on this plan—would have involved no more than a few months' delay for the developers in completing some tawdry restaurant facility, but Kido had been overruled, alas. As on many previous occasions. When? Oh, no more than a couple of weeks ago, and no doubt the developers had already obliterated the piece of land concerned.

Mr Araki would obviously have been more than happy to go on for a couple of hours, but Otani thanked him warmly, and excused himself with real regret. He had to move on to talk to Zenji Ono, and had some quick thinking to do in the car on the way, because something puzzled him. It wasn't that the boring time-server who saw him first had launched into a long defensive speech. That was quite understandable. The fellow almost certainly had a guilty conscience. He was of an age to be thinking of retirement and was probably planning a relatively modest 'descent from heaven' of the kind accomplished on the grand scale by senior national civil servants. They retired at fifty-five, pocketed their lavish lump sums and pensions from public funds and then within a matter of weeks reappeared as directors of companies their former ministries had dealt with. Small fry had ambitions too, and the prefectural official might well have wangled the planning approval for Zenji Ono in the expectation of going to work for him in due course at a fat salary. But why, if Kido's objections to Ono's company's plans to build over the site of the former temple had in fact been overruled, was he *then* murdered by the paper-maker Miyamoto on the instructions of Ono's gangster friends?

Seventeen

Otani left the plush offices of the Elite Property Development Company feeling rather pleased with himself. His mood abruptly changed to one of anxiety when his driver Tomita spotted him coming out of the building, leapt from the car and told him that he was needed urgently at headquarters.

'From Inspector Hara's office, you say? When did you get the radio message?'

'Only four minutes ago, sir. I was going to give you one more minute and then come in after you.' By this time they were already on the move, and for only the third or fourth time in over ten years Tomita had activated the siren and was cleaving a way through the heavy lunchtime traffic, covering the distance of about a mile to police headquarters in less than three minutes, a miraculous achievement for central Kobe. Tomita had been given no clue as to why Otani had been summoned, and for that reason Otani decided not to use the car phone to try to find out for himself.

Hara was in any case waiting, grim-faced, at the top of the steps. On seeing the car he came down to the kerbside and opened the rear door for Otani the moment Tomita brought the car to a squealing halt.

'Bad news from Anraku-in, sir. The summer school secretary's been murdered. Kimura's on his way there now by car, and I think I should go too. I waited to ask you if you wished—'

'To go with you? No. I have things to talk to Ninja about. Take my car. Tomita! Drive Inspector Hara to Sasayama right away, and keep that siren going as long as necessary. Anything else I need to know immediately, Hara?'

'Two things, sir. Neither of them good. Woman Senior Detective Migishima has submitted her resignation to me over the phone, and insists she'll be confirming it in writing immediately. And I'm afraid Miyamoto's probably not our man. Inspector Noguchi will fill you in.'

'Understood. Get in the car, and call in with a situation report when you can. On your way, Tomita.'

*

'Original name was Asano. Respectable family background. Father owned a high class stationery shop, dealt direct with two or three well-known makers, including this bloke in Kyushu name of Miyamoto. Young Asano tried his hand at paper-making as boy. Miyamoto saw some of his work on a visit to Osaka, quite impressed, offered to take the lad as an apprentice.'

Otani groaned, made a fist and thumped his forehead with his knuckles. 'No need to go on, Ninja. The boy turned out to be the master's favourite student, and when the old man wanted to retire he adopted him and gave him his own name as his successor. It's a very common practice in artistic and craft circles and I could kick myself for not even thinking of it this time.'

'Ah well, can't win 'em all. Anyway, no connection with my garbage man.'

Otani sat back in his chair, closed his eyes and exhaled noisily. 'What a mess. Right back to square one, plus a brand-new murder on our hands. And what's all this non-sense about Junko Migishima resigning? Surely she'd talk to you first before doing something like that?' Noguchi had after all acted as go-between when the Migishimas were married, and therefore ought to be consulted over any important matter likely to affect their lives.

'We'll talk her out of it one way or another, Hara and me. Kid blames herself for this latest killing, see? Apparently she was talking to your wife's sister, thought they were alone but a snooper was listening in. Junko-chan reckons she pointed the finger at the Yasuda girl as being key witness in the Kido case. Whoever was on the other side of the door went straight to Yasuda's office and stopped her mouth for good. Strangled the girl, or maybe used a judo killer hold, something like that.'

'Poor girl. She was so bright, too. I remember suggesting we ought to try to recruit her. Anyway, we're not accepting any Migishima resignation, and that's flat. Who found the body?'

'Your sister-in-law. When they realised they'd been overheard she went to find the Yasuda girl while Junko-chan got on the phone to Hara. S'pose they had the idea of putting her under protection. Unless, that is,' Noguchi added slowly, 'it was your sister-in-law that did her in.'

Otani's mouth opened in outrage, and Noguchi raised a meaty hand to stay him. 'No point in flying off the handle. I don't believe it for a minute, but it's got to be considered.'

*

'Is that you, Kimura? Yes, Ninja passed on the essentials, I think. Yes, it's a very bad business, and I'm sorry for all concerned. Make sure Hara keeps Junko Migishima busy, won't you. Kimura, I want you personally to get a statement from Michiko Yanagida, my sister-in-law. Not Hara. What? How do I know what to think? It's totally bewildering to have to start all over again when I thought we were on the point of getting everything cut and dried. I may or may not have had a useful morning, I'll fill you all in on that when we next meet. Right, now I know you've all got plenty to do, so I'll ring off and let you get on.' Otani made to break the connection, then hastily began to speak again.

'Kimura? Still there? Good. This nearly slipped my mind in all the confusion. It might be worth looking into one little point I picked up today. From the secretary of the archaeological advisory panel Kido used to chair. It seems that when he was much younger Kido made his name as an archaeologist by unearthing a valuable Buddha image of some kind. Hollow, and with a twelfth-century scroll inside. The man I spoke to mentioned that Kido had a gaijin research associate at the time. I'm wondering if it could by any chance have been the American fellow – was his name Ashby? Oh, *Ashree* was it? My mistake. I could check with the man at the prefectural office, but it might be more discreet for you to do it from your end. I'm still convinced I'm right about how Kido was murdered, so I suppose the paper expert stays on the list as a suspect, but my theory about the motive has gone right down the drain. You said this Ashree man has been knocking about Japan for a very long time. If he worked with Kido as a young man, I suppose he might have had some reason to kill him. What? Well don't ask me, man. Use your imagination. Perhaps they fell in love with the same woman. Perhaps Ashree resented seeing Kido get all the academic glory for their discovery and becoming a famous professor while he looks like ending up as a PR odd-job man for a crazy religious sect. At all events, if he's dealt in Japanese prints and so forth he might quite likely have heard about the wet washi murder technique. There seems to be no great secret about it, surprisingly enough.'

*

'Oh yes, it was some time in the fifties, I believe,' Philippa Kilpeck said. 'Long before my time, of course, but articles appearing in archaeological and medieval history journals nowadays still quite often contain references to the Kitano Buddha.'

'What was so special about it?' Since this was official

150

business, Kimura spoke from the straight chair to which he had been banished, while Philippa sat on the edge of her bed.

'Be reasonable, Jiro. It's miles outside my specialised field. I could look it up for you if there were any relevant English language reference books here, but there aren't. Thank you for confiding in me, anyway. I can see that it's out of the question for you to ask the man himself, but I don't think I can be of much help. I have only the vaguest idea why people got so excited when the Buddha was discovered near Kobe all those years ago. Something about its being the only example so far found of a hollow image with a written scroll inside, as distinct from coiled silk braids symbolising entrails, I fancy. That, and the fact that nothing of any real importance had been discovered in that area, compared with the treasures unearthed near Nara and Kyoto, even Osaka.'

'Well, at least you've explained how it made Kido's name.'

'Don't go by what I say, for goodness' sake. There are experts at the National Museum in Kyoto who could be consulted. Or if you can't wait, Professor Yanagida would certainly know more than I do. It's not her field either, but she was on friendly terms with Professor Kido and probably took an informed interest in his work.'

'She's kind of upset, Philippa.'

'Of course. Poor woman. What a ghastly experience for her.'

'A lot ghastlier for Shoko Yasuda.'

'That's an insufferable thing to say! Do you imagine I'm not aware of that?' Having flared up at Kimura, Philippa glared at him for a moment with clenched fists before breaking down, sobbing. Kimura moved to her side and put an arm round her shoulders, squeezing gently until her stiff resistance broke down and she slumped against him.

'I'm sorry. Truly sorry,' he said then. 'You've all been

under a terrible strain. But I think it's almost over now. Thanks to what you've told me. Hara and I will go and see Ashley now, and with any luck he'll be able to give us the last piece of the jig-saw.'

*

While they were inside the main building talking to Ashley the sky had darkened and it had rained, briefly but heavily, for the first time in over two weeks. So there was a washed, cool freshness in the air when Hara and Kimura went out of the emergency door at the back of the building and strolled towards the residential blocks. 'Well, you're the English speaker,' Hara said. 'Do you think he was telling the truth?'

Kimura nodded. 'I do, yes. At first he didn't want to, but he was relieved once he got started.' He stopped short and turned to face Hara. 'Where's Junko Migishima?'

'With Michiko. Professor Yanagida, I mean. You know, I can't believe that the superintendent seriously thought her capable of killing that girl. His own wife's sister.'

'Don't be naive, Hara. Every murderer's somebody's relative, after all. I doubt if the chief did consider the idea seriously, but she had to be questioned. It was theoretically possible for her to have done it. By her own account she volunteered to go and find Shoko Yasuda immediately after hearing her described as a key witness. The intruder in the auditorium was almost certainly the murderer of both Kido and the girl, but Professor Yanagida could have got there before him. Nice for you to know she's off the hook now, anyway. Well, what are you going to do about her, Hara?'

'I don't intrude into your private affairs,' Hara said huffily, 'and I see no reason why—'

'I'm not talking about the professor. Junko, I mean. She can't possibly to be allowed to resign.'

'I agree. But she is in a very low state of mind. As I imagine you or I would be in her position.'

'Sure. I have an idea, though, now that we're pretty sure

of our man. A bit of a long shot, and we'll need Professor Yanagida's cooperation if it's to work. Think she might help?'

'If I ask her to she will,' Hara said with quiet confidence. 'What do you have in mind?'

*

'*Ohairi kudasai.*' The Japanese invitation to enter sounded as friendly as it was courteous, and Michiko Yanagida sagged with fear and apprehension. What if Takeshi Hara was utterly mistaken? How on earth could she endure the humiliation if he was innocent of these dreadful crimes? But then, how much greater the humiliation if she were to fail the first test of her faith in this new man in her life? She straightened herself, opened the door and stepped inside.

'Professor Yanagida! What a pleasant surprise. Come in, come in and sit down. Be so good as to close the door, the shower has lowered the temperature and I am very susceptible to draughts.'

Michiko omitted all the customary courtesies normally used by women speaking Japanese, and employed the language in its plainest masculine form. 'What I have to say will not please you, but there is no point in my beating about the bush. I saw you follow me and the young policewoman this morning, and I know that you overheard our conversation from inside the auditorium. From the dais I saw your unmistakeable silhouette as you slipped out, and I reached the downstairs corridor just in time to see you leave the building. Seconds after you killed Shoko Yasuda.'

'Did you indeed? Well, well. What an observant lady you are, to be sure.'

'I'm also very determined, and short of money. Otherwise I'd have told the police already. For the moment I'm the only person who knows the truth about this affair and I could be persuaded to hold my tongue. But it will cost you . . . shall we say five million yen? Not even as much as a year's salary. A bargain.'

'My dear colleague, you have obviously taken leave of your senses. A person of my international standing a murderer? Do you really imagine anyone would believe such a thing for a second? You'll not get five yen of mine, much less five million. I am on the point of leaving this ridiculous establishment. There are my bags, standing on the floor, ready packed. Within fifteen minutes they and I will be in a hire car being driven to Osaka International Airport.'

Inspiration was very slow to come, but twenty years of experience in the cut-throat world of university teaching had taught Michiko more than she realised, and after an agonising few seconds when her brain seemed to have seized up completely, she found herself in possession of the perfect goad. 'That will do you no good,' she said with a calmness she was far from feeling. 'Because you're worse than a murderer. You're an academic fraud, and I shall denounce you as such in the *International Journal of Archaeology*, just as Professor Kido was planning to do.'

Kimura had warned her that the man was dangerous, probably insane, and that having killed twice he would have no compunction about attacking her. Nevertheless when it came to the point she froze with terror, and managed only a feeble croak when strong hands encircled her neck and the terrible pressure began. She was near enough to the door to kick it, however, and it flew open to admit Junko Migishima.

*

'Don't fuss, Hara. Remember Junko's an *aikido* black belt. And had specialist training in unarmed combat when she was assigned as a bodyguard to Margaret Thatcher in Tokyo. Let her have a bit of a run for her money.' Kimura took out his trashy Sesame Street watch and waited for another ten seconds. 'All right, let's go and pull him in,' he said then, and set off along the corridor. A few moments later the two inspectors contemplated the scene inside the room.

'*Bonsoir, M'sieu Leclerc*,' Kimura said. '*Evidemment vous êtes déjà saisi.*' It was perfectly obvious, but Kimura very seldom had an opportunity to show off his French.

In the circumstances he was understandably annoyed when Michiko Yanagida completely upstaged him by flinging herself into Hara's arms and clinging to him, shuddering, while he murmured awkward endearments to her.

Eighteen

'She was in complete control of the situation,' Kimura said. 'When we got there she had Leclerc face down on the floor in an armlock, and Professor Yanagida was getting his belt off to use to tie his wrists behind his back.'

'And how did it come about that Woman Senior Detective Migishima was so conveniently on hand to come to the aid of my sister-in-law?' Otani enquired. 'I ask merely because it might occur to the district prosecutor to do so when I make my submission to him.' Otani was in little doubt that Kimura and Hara had entered into some sort of conspiracy to arrange for Junko's morale to be restored following the death of Shoko Yasuda. Since they had evidently succeeded, he was quite willing to accept that the ends – namely the arrest of the French professor and the withdrawal of Junko's resignation – justified the means, provided they could be explained away plausibly enough.

Hara bravely took up the challenge. 'Officer Migishima made an oral report to me while Inspector Kimura was accompanying Leclerc to the Sasayama police station lock-up. She stated that Professor Yanagida had approached her shortly before the incident, and told her she had suspected for some time that Leclerc might have had a hand in the so-called accidents that befell Professor Kido before his death. Professor Yanagida herself confirmed to me that this conversation had taken place.'

'I'll bet she did. Go on, Hara.'

'After the shock of discovering Shoko Yasuda's body she tried to remember who'd been about earlier and might have seen her and Officer Migishima going into the main building. She recalled noticing Leclerc standing there on his own in the open space between the buildings at the relevant time. Very rashly as it turned out, Professor Yanagida decided to go to his room and tackle Leclerc – who speaks near-perfect Japanese, incidentally – on the subject, and announced her intention to Officer Migishima—'

'Who, in spite of her own distress of mind, decided to follow and stand by in case of need. Not bad, Hara, but it'll need quite a bit of polishing when you put all this in writing. Be particularly careful over the chronology. It might look bad if the prosecutor were to get the wrong idea. For instance, that before this significant exchange took place you and Hara had already spoken to the American and decided you had enough to justify pulling Leclerc in.' Otani shook his head sadly. 'I'm sorry to say that the prosecutor's a bit of a cynic. He might just possibly be misguided enough to suspect that the pair of you put my sister-in-law up to this.'

'Not a chance, Chief,' Kimura said breezily. 'The prosecutor wouldn't dare to question the word of a person like Professor Yanagida. Japanese women aren't inclined to let themselves be pushed around any more these days. Why don't you check with her yourself?'

'I'm shocked to hear you suggest such a thing. It would be highly improper for me to interview a close relative in an official context. If anybody's going to put words in her mouth I'd prefer it not to be me. The prosecutor may decide to ask to see her. In fact I rather hope he will. I'm quite sure she'd be more than a match for him.'

'Finished your fun and games?' It was Noguchi who butted in, a sour look on his battered face. 'I thought we were still supposed to be sorting out a couple of murders.'

Otani at once abandoned his bantering manner. 'You're

quite right, Ninja. I'm sorry. All right, gentlemen. In the matter of the Anraku-in murders, responsibility for the tidying-up operation falls to you, Kimura. Whether or not he confesses, get some sort of formal statement out of Leclerc in French and have it translated into Japanese and attested. Liaise with the French consular authorities, warn the other gaijin up there that we shall take a poor view of any gossiping on their part, generally sort out the foreign complications. You know the drill.'

He turned to Hara. 'Right, no fooling. You'll caution and interview my sister-in-law in the presence of another responsible officer, one not already acquainted with her. Her statement has got to be absolutely watertight. It might not be necessary to spell out inessential details, but whatever she does go on record as saying has got to be literally true, and unchallengeable. Understood?'

'Yes, sir.'

'You'll also prepare the summary of evidence and a first draft of our submission to the district prosecutor for me. I don't think it would be appropriate for me to see Officer Migishima myself at this stage, but you may recommend a commendation if you see fit. And needless to say, I have heard nothing about any talk of resignation.'

'Understood. Thank you, sir.'

'Now then, as Ninja Noguchi has just reminded us, there is still a great deal of other business demanding our attention. Specifically, the killing in Osaka of the low-grade informer Miyamoto, and the disappearance of Keizo Hosoda. I have some information to share with you as a consequence of the calls I made yesterday at the prefectural planning department's offices and on Zenji Ono. Remember that I was at the time still under the impression that I knew who had killed Kido, and more or less why; and that I was of course completely wrong on both counts.'

'But nevertheless there was a connection, as we now know.'

'Thank you for the courtesy, Kimura, but that has been established much more by luck than by the judgment of any of us. Before I kick off, explain to us all again, briefly, how the case against Leclerc took shape.'

Kimura took a deep breath. 'Shoko Yasuda was killed yesterday morning. As soon as word was received here, I went to Anraku-in. Hara followed soon after. You rang me there in the afternoon, mentioning that you'd been hearing about Kido's archaeological find back in the fifties. And that he'd had a gaijin research associate. You wondered if it might have been Ashley, who's not a scholar but has lived in Japan for many years and is very knowledgeable about Japanese culture and history. I consulted Dr Kilpeck, the British historian, and she said no, it was Professor Maximilian Leclerc who had worked with Kido as a young postgraduate and kept in touch with him ever since.'

'And that Leclerc had got just as much career advantage in France out of their discovery as Kido did here, right?'

'Yes. Now we knew from your sister-in-law that something serious was bothering Ashley. She thought he was on the edge of a nervous breakdown, in fact, and Hara and I found him in a very precarious state. Remember his secretary had been killed only a few hours earlier. Once he realised we knew about Leclerc's history, Ashley admitted having himself been acquainted with both Kido and Leclerc for over thirty years. I pressed him hard, and he let slip that early this year Kido got drunk in his company and took him into his confidence. By confessing to Ashley that the famous Kitano Buddha that had made his and Leclerc's names was a fake.'

'Two young men could fool the academic community that easily?'

'I don't pretend to understand the technical details, Chief. Maybe thirty-odd years ago scientific tests weren't anything like as sophisticated as they are now.'

'The academic establishment can still be fooled, sir,'

Hara put in. 'A distinguished British historian was taken in completely a few years ago by a German con-man who claimed to have found Hitler's personal diaries.'

'All right, I'll take your word for it. Go on, Kimura.'

'Anyway, it seems that Kido's conscience troubled him more and more as he got older and accomplished some genuinely good work, and he wanted to come clean. But that would have meant exposing Leclerc too. Kido tried the idea of a joint statement on Leclerc, arguing that they were both eminent enough to survive the scandal, but Leclerc's a much more arrogant man and wouldn't hear of it. Quite the reverse. He came here and bullied and threatened Kido, staging those incidents to let Kido know what would happen to him if he opened his mouth. That was why Kido himself tried to keep his mishaps as quiet as possible, and urged Ashley to play them down too.'

'The American doesn't seem to have played a very heroic role in all this.'

'Maybe not, but he was in a very invidious position, after all. The success of this first international summer school meant a lot to him, and given that Kido himself was pretending to stay on good terms with Leclerc, Ashley didn't take much persuading not to rock the boat. He claimed to us that he honestly thought Kido had in effect worried himself into a heart attack, or even committed suicide in despair. He basically wanted to contain any scandal and get Leclerc and the rest of the gaijin off the Anraku-in premises as quickly and quietly as possible. Which is why he blamed poor Shoko Yasuda for stirring things up.'

'You were there, Hara. Do you go along with Kimura's interpretation of all this?'

'I do. And subject to whatever Leclerc himself has to say, it seems to be a tenable hypothesis that the worm turned, as it were. At the end of his tether, Kido told Leclerc that he was going to confess to the fraud anyway, and Leclerc therefore decided he had to be silenced. He is quite expert enough about things Japanese to have known about the wet washi murder method.'

'Well, if that's the best we can do, so be it. It's all hearsay and I hope to goodness we'll get a confession. Where is this bogus Buddha now, by the way?'

'I don't know. Some museum, presumably.'

'Well, someone must find out, and get the experts to take a good hard state-of-the-art look at it. If it can be clearly proved to be a fake and the Frenchman's as touchy about his reputation as you suggest, it ought to well and truly jolt his composure.' Otani looked at his watch. 'We've spent quite long enough on this. Now we really must get on to the problem of Hosoda.'

*

Twenty minutes later Otani was still talking. Glossing over his pointless interview with the planning official, he had given the other three a full account of the conversation with Araki, the enthusiastic secretary of the archaeological advisory panel, and moved on to his meeting with Zenji Ono.

'I'd seen him before, of course, fussing before the lunch they gave for Hosoda at the Nara Hotel. On that occasion he was behaving like a pompous little organiser, and I took him for one of the gang's more educated flunkeys. It was an eye-opener to see him in his own fancy office. Very much in charge, huge desk, and as cool as a cucumber, at first. I imagine he'd had a phone call from his place-man in the planning department immediately after I left, and thought I'd been nicely brain-washed. He showed me all his glossy brochures, plans and flow-charts, and at one point I thought he was going to offer to sell me one of the Royal Heights apartments at a huge discount – what are you looking so wistful about, Kimura?'

'Me, Chief? Oh, nothing. It *is* a fantastic development, though.'

'That's a matter of opinion, but if I ever find out you've

moved there on your pay it'll mean a court of enquiry, I warn you. Anyway, when I thought Ono was well off his guard, I asked him when he'd last seen Keizo Hosoda.'

'Shook him rigid, did you?'

'Yes, I think you could fairly say that, Ninja. He went as white as a sheet, started sweating and tried to cover it up by muttering something about eating something that disagreed with him. Actually went so far as to excuse himself and went into what was obviously his private washroom. Which gave me an opportunity to have a closer look at the flow-charts recording the progress of the building work, and a peep at his desk diary. Ono came back two or three minutes later full of apologies, having pulled himself together somewhat. I think he'd been throwing up.'

'What did he say about Hosoda, sir?'

'Not a word, and I tactfully abandoned any idea of pursuing the subject. It seemed unnecessary in the circumstances. So I merely thanked Ono for giving me his time, hoped he'd feel better soon and congratulated him on having finally got an official permit to complete the last bit of the development. Then I bowed and walked out, leaving a very worried man behind me. Ninja, I've been talking far too much. Will you bring us up to date?'

'Not much to tell. I went over to the site late yesterday in my day labourer's gear, got hold of a hard hat and took a good look round the place. Saw where they'd got busy on the restaurant annex since last week. On the bit of land they'd been held up over by Kido. Come knocking-off time, got talking to some of the lads. A few drinks, you know how it is.'

'Thank you, Ninja.' Having drunk a cup of chilled green tea, Otani took up the story again himself. 'I had been able to give Ninja certain information about dates and times last week, gleaned from the material in Ono's office. He was able to confirm from his conversations that all the supervisory staff at the site – but no top brass from the office –

were attending an hour-long meeting in the afternoon of a particular day. An afternoon that, according to his office diary, Ono had kept clear of engagements. The only entry was "Out on private business". Later that same afternoon, the concrete was poured for the restaurant floor. Tell me, gentlemen, are you all thinking what I'm thinking?' There was a pause while they all looked at each other, and then Kimura spoke.

'Well, I am for one. But you'll never get permission, Chief.'

'Oh, I wouldn't be too sure of that. Look at it this way. Those two yakuza barons Takeuchi and Ikeda thought Ono was going to be a bigger asset to them than Hosoda, which is why they wanted Hosoda removed. Now they're not so sure. They've already been put to the inconvenience of having to have an informer disposed of in an embarrassingly public way, to the annoyance of the formidable Inspector Noguchi and the commander of the Osaka prefectural police force. Ninja and I have talked it over, and we're inclined to think they might be ready to give us Ono as a peace offering.'

Nineteen

The evening was softly warm, with the merest hint of a breeze ruffling the surface of the dully glittering Kamo river in Kyoto. The moon had risen about half an hour earlier, and was sufficiently near the full to outshine the lighted windows in the buildings lining the opposite bank, and even to offer some competition to the paper lanterns illuminating the open-air restaurant platform built out over the water on the Pontocho side. There Philippa Kilpeck and Jiro Kimura were lingering over coffee and brandy.

'It's beautiful, Jiro. Thank you for bringing me here.'

'It's all right after dark, when you can't see the TV aerials and electricity supply lines on the other side so easily. You can imagine what it must have been like in the old days.'

'Yes. There are still geisha working here, aren't there?'

'Oh, sure. That narrow street outside was once full of geisha houses, and there are still a good few left. You can bet there are a dozen or more geisha parties going on within a hundred yards of us right now.' Kimura cocked his head, listening to the sounds of laughter and snatches of song coming from similar riverside dining platforms to either side of them, and looked apologetic. 'Maybe I should have tried to organise one for you, but I must admit I'd rather have you to myself.'

'Don't be silly. I'm having a wonderful time, and besides, I've been given some idea how much a geisha party costs. Strictly an expense account luxury, I believe. I'm a very practical lady, Jiro.' She reached across and squeezed his hand. 'Everyone was most impressed by your speech to us foreigners before the summer school broke up.'

'You must be kidding. I was terrified, standing up there in front of all you intellectuals.' He sighed. 'Well, it turned out to be a pretty lousy vacation course, didn't it? Ashley's talking about organising another one next year, but I somehow doubt if he'll be able to get it off the ground once the word gets around overseas that people tend to get themselves killed at Anraku-in.'

'Not a bit of it. Not so far as the westerners are concerned, anyway, take it from me. Most of us haven't had so much excitement for years. The rumour's gone round that Michiko Yanagida may be the academic director next year, and everybody likes her. Maggie Threlfall will certainly be back, probably having recruited other Australians. She's convinced herself that she was mainly responsible for Max Leclerc's downfall, so she's developed a proprietary interest in the future of the summer school. Besides, she fancies Bill Ashley, you know.'

'Does she, now?'

'And I'll be back, because . . . oh, for a number of reasons.'

'Really ? That's great news!' Kimura gazed at her fondly, noticing yet again how cleverly she rang the changes on what must inevitably have been a comparatively restricted wardrobe. The open jacket and sleeveless top were what she had worn for their last visit to Kyoto, but were transformed by the black and oyster silk Liberty scarf flung loosely round her neck, and the jet, pearl and gold earrings and necklace. Not to mention the full black skirt and high-heeled shoes. A snappy dresser himself, he appreciated her flair. 'It calls for more brandy.'

'Not for me, thank you. If I arrive back at the Kyoto Ladies' Hotel tiddly, they'll never let me in. Anyway, I was telling you about us gaijin. Even Manfred Weisse—'

'The German sourpuss?'

'He's not, you know. Not now, anyway. He really is a very distinguished calligrapher, and it turns out that he's had his doubts about the authenticity of the Kitano Buddha scroll for years. The image itself is genuine enough, he told me, but wouldn't have generated anything like so much excitement in academic circles as it did at the time if it hadn't been for the scroll that Leclerc and Kido claimed to have found inside. Manfred can't stand Leclerc – he *is* an insufferable man quite apart from the dreadful things he seems to have done – and he's delighted to think he's about to be exposed as a fraud.'

'Gee whiz, I shall never understand scholars. Are you saying your German friend reckons the fraud's more important than the murders?'

'Perhaps, when there's a Sorbonne professorship in Japanese art history at stake and Manfred Weisse's bound to be one of the strongest candidates for it. Don't look so shocked. I told you I'm a practical lady.'

Kimura shook his head from side to side, smiling ruefully. 'You sure are. I'd better change the subject. Explain something that's been puzzling me, will you? I've now spent several hours in Leclerc's company. I agree he's an arrogant man. Or was, anyway. Pathetic would be a better word for him now that he's heard what the experts at the National Museum have discovered about his famous scroll. That the paper dates from at least two hundred years after the Buddha was buried, I mean. But darn it, Philippa, he's in his late fifties, has white hair, leans on a stick when he walks. How in the world could he have fixed up that booby-trap at the Hiyoshi Taisha? Or shot that arrow through the window at Kido?'

'Oh, that's easy. The silver-topped stick's a pure affectation, good for his image as the aristocratic scholar. And hasn't Bill Ashley told you that Max Leclerc was quite a martial arts expert in his day? Michiko Yanagida for one can vouch for how strong he is. He'd have had no problem at the shrine. He wandered off on his own almost as soon as we got off the bus, and would have been familiar with the normal sightseeing route. So he would have been able to take a short cut and gain several minutes on us. It's common knowledge even among people like me that all those old wooden shrine buildings were constructed without nails. Leclerc of all people would have known just what pegs to tap out of place to make that particular structure dangerous.'

'Without even getting out of breath, no doubt.'

'You're teasing me.'

'Do you mind?'

'Not really. You look tired, Jiro. Are the French consular people giving you a hard time?'

'Oh, I'm used to that kind of hassle. It's my job.'

'All the same, I think I'll go back to the hotel now, and let you get home.'

'I'd rather—'

'No you wouldn't. You must be exhausted. And remember you've invited me to come and dine at your flat in Kobe the day after tomorrow. The evening before I leave Osaka for Hong Kong and back to London. I, um, well, I've told the hotel I shall be checking out that day.'

*

'Don't be silly, I shall enjoy the stroll,' Otani insisted over both women's protests. 'It isn't all that often that you come to the house and stay for supper with us. The least I can do is see you to Rokko Station.' He slipped into his shoes and walked out of the front door to the outer gate, remembering too late that Michiko and Hanae had only just begun the protracted business of saying goodbye to each other, and that he was probably in for a wait of several minutes.

No matter. It was good to smell the evening air, look at the moon and see the shaggy bulk of the Rokko hills looming not far away. He smiled to himself, thinking back over the evening. He hadn't been best pleased to arrive home after a demanding day of bureaucratic politicking to find Michiko there, but there was no doubt that she was a lot easier to get on with these days than ever before that he could remember. Chatty, good-humoured, and properly sympathetic about the problems of getting anything done in a hurry through official channels. Scrupulous, too, in avoiding any discussion of her part in the entrapment of the Frenchman. Hara had obviously briefed her carefully and well.

He burped discreetly. Hanae had surpassed herself, too. Not only jumbo prawns in ginger sauce to accompany the rice, but breaded pork cutlets to follow, washed down with plenty of sake. Delicious. More suitable in theory for a chilly autumn evening than late August perhaps, but Hanae knew his favourites.

'Sorry to have kept you waiting.'

'Not at all, you haven't been long, and I've been enjoying looking at the moon.' They fell into step side by side, Otani setting a leisurely pace along the street, round the corner and down the hill. 'I'm afraid I can't remember the times, but it's not even half-past nine yet, so there are still trains every quarter of an hour. Even if we just miss one you won't have long to wait.'

'That's right.'

'I've enjoyed your company this evening, Michiko. I hope this invitation to you to take over next year as academic director of the summer school does materialise.'

'So do I.'

She hadn't been so uncommunicative earlier, Otani thought, and tried again. 'You aren't superstitious? Don't think there's a curse on the project, anything like that?'

'Good gracious, no! If I do get the job, I shall plan to double its size within three years and really put the summer school on the map. From an international point of view, I mean.'

'I don't doubt it for a moment. You'll make a very dynamic director, I'm sure. Anything wrong? Twisted your ankle?'

'No, no.' Having been lagging a little behind, Michiko stopped altogether. 'Look, there's absolutely no need for you to go all the way to the station with me.'

'No bother, I assure you. We're over half way there anyway.'

'The fact is, well, I don't want to seem rude, but the fact is, I'm meeting a friend, you see. So I'd just as soon say goodnight here, if you don't mind.'

'Oh, I'm so sorry. Stupid of me. Of course, of course. I'll leave you here, then. Off you go. See you again soon, I hope.'

'I hope so too. It was a very pleasant evening. Thank you. Goodnight, Tetsuo.'

Then Michiko was hurrying off, with Otani gazing after her dumbstruck. Not because he realised that she must have arranged a late rendezvous with Hara at Rokko Station, but because it was the very first time she had ever called him Tetsuo.

*

Hanae was finishing off the dishes when he arrived home again.

'Hello, you're soon back.'

Otani lounged in the kitchen doorway and studied her. 'Yes. She was in too much of a hurry for me, so I didn't go all the way to the station with her. That was a delicious supper. I ate too much. Better wait half an hour or so before I have my bath. Did you and Michiko have a good chat before I got home?'

'What do you think? Want to know all about it?'

He contorted his face into one of the ferocious kabuki scowls that always made her laugh. 'I'd quite like to, but I don't think I'd better,' he said when she had subsided. 'I resisted the temptation to follow her to the station to see who she was meeting there, after all.'

'I did try to talk you out of going in the first place. It isn't all that hard to guess, is it?'

'No, but guesswork's one thing, having to face hard facts something else. So leave me at least partly in the dark, will you? By the way, the most extraordinary thing happened.'

'Oh? What?'

'She called me Tetsuo. Even you hardly ever do that. What do you make of it?'

Hanae took off her apron and Otani made way for her, following her into the living room. There she turned to face him, and took his hands in hers. 'I expect it was because she's a lot more fond of you than she's ever been willing to admit before. Oh, and I might have happened to mention to her in passing that I was giving you a special supper, because I know you're a bit anxious about tomorrow.' She leaned forward and kissed him on the cheek.

'I'll remember to have the whisky out, ready for when you come home. Good luck, darling Tetsuo.'

Twenty

The district prosecutor had specified that the operation should be carried out as unobtrusively as possible, so after a brief early rendezvous at headquarters, Otani and a distinctly puffy-eyed Hara took an ordinary taxi from there to the Kobe Royal Heights building site, arriving just before seven in the morning. It promised to be another very warm day, but they were soberly suited. Noguchi was already there, waiting for them outside the checker's office at the main gate. Otani had quite expected him to be wearing his day labourer's disguise of a scruffy T-shirt, breeches with a purple woollen belly-band showing above the waist, and rubber-soled footwear with a separate compartment for the big toe; but in fact Noguchi had got hold of a pair of foreman's white overalls with the logo of the Elite Property Development Company on the breast pocket and looked quite distinguished in them, especially when he put a hard hat on after handing them one each.

'Are we supposed to put coveralls on too, Ninja?'

'Not yet, just the helmets. We'll get you some later if you feel like joining in. Prosecutor's coming at half past, right?'

'Yes. He insisted on being present, as he has a perfect right to be. Oh, and there'll be a man called Araki arriving about the same time, to represent the prefectural archaeological advisory committee. I'd better greet the prosecutor here myself.'

' 'F you say so. Come and meet the site manager first. I've talked to him – decent guy, I'm pretty sure he's in the clear over all this himself. Rumours flying round all over the place, needless to say, but he's going to keep people well away from our end. Main shift don't start till eight anyway. Your two lads are up there already, Hara. OK, let's go.'

Physically, there wasn't a great deal to show as a result of two days of intensive negotiations that had called for every ploy and technique Otani had learned in his long years of experience as a senior public official. There was no love lost between him and the wily district prosecutor, and it hadn't been easy to persuade him to entertain the idea in the first place; and that was only the beginning.

There had also been the chairman of the Prefectural Public Safety Commission to soften up, and through him several key members of the prefectural governor's official entourage, as well as a couple of people at City Hall. In building their successful careers all these worthies had been guided by the Japanese proverb that it's the nail that sticks up that gets hammered, and none was eager to accept personal responsibility. However, by suggesting subtly to each in turn that there was already a consensus, Otani had finally managed to manoeuvre them into a position where to dissent would have made any one of them look more conspicuous than to agree.

Meantime, Noguchi had been doing equally tricky business with the gangster barons Takeuchi and Ikeda, involving a good deal of give and take on both sides before an acceptable bargain was made. Noguchi had been obliged to give certain assurances about the restraints the police would observe in investigating the affairs of Zenji Ono as they related to those of the yakuza syndicate, while the gangsters undertook in return to guarantee not only to produce Ono on demand but also that there would be no interference with the evidence. A great deal had to be taken on trust and things could still go horribly wrong, but Noguchi insisted that there was no other way to handle such a delicate situation.

Hara had ventured to recommend otherwise, but in spite of his misgivings no police guard had been mounted over the restaurant annex site even after the order was given for a halt to the building work there, and it was a team of ordinary workmen who were standing by with pneumatic drills and earth-moving equipment when Otani and his companions arrived to be greeted by the site manager.

Otani handed him the formal demolition order finally issued by the prefectural planning department the previous afternoon, the manager gave the word and immediately the drills were at work, making the morning hideous with their noise. Otani left Hara and Noguchi, now equipped with ear-pads, to keep an eye on things, and returned to the main gate.

He was just in time to rescue Mr Araki the archaeological enthusiast. It wasn't altogether surprising that the checker now on duty at the open window of his shed viewed him with suspicion. Araki looked if anything rather more odd out of doors than he had in his office, dressed as he was in the top half of a conventional suit, but with faded blue jeans below and canvas trainer shoes on his large feet. Moreover, he seemed to be trying to explain his presence by trying to interest the morose checker in the ancient history of the area rather than by producing anything in the way of credentials.

'Good morning, Mr Araki. I'm very glad to meet you again. It's all right,' Otani added, turning to the man in the shed. 'This gentleman's with me.' A glossy black Nissan Bluebird drew up behind them. 'Oh, and here's the other one I was expecting.'

Grumbling to himself, the checker rummaged in the shed behind him and found two more plastic helmets. He thrust them out through the window. 'Expected or not, they don't get past me without one o' these.'

District Prosecutor Akamatsu approached, wearing his habitual expression of quizzical disdain, his mouth open to form an O-shape that concealed his teeth. The habit had led to his being referred to by many of those who had dealings with him as the Black Hole.

'Good morning, Mr Prosecutor.'

'Good morning, Superintendent,' Akamatsu said, ignoring the beaming Araki. 'I have instructed my driver to return to the office.'

Otani wasn't quite sure what he was supposed to say to that, but was determined to see the civilities observed. 'Mr Prosecutor, this is Mr Araki, who is an official of the planning department of the prefectural government and permanent secretary to the archaeological advisory committee. Right-hand man to the late Professor Kido.'

The prosecutor, himself dressed in an immaculate dark suit, stared pointedly at Araki's jeans and nodded curtly, but didn't bother to address him. Irritated, Otani shoved one of the helmets at Akamatsu and handed the other with ostentatious politeness to the archaeologist. 'Please put these on, and follow me.'

Unabashed by having been snubbed, or more probably unaware of the fact, Araki babbled happily about the history of the site all the way to the restaurant area. Otani listened with interest and put in the occasional comment or question, and made no attempt to address the prosecutor again until they were nearly there. Then he turned to him.

'It would have been impossible to hear ourselves think while the concrete was being broken up, so I authorised them to go ahead with the drilling in the small area involved before you arrived. Needless to say, the operation was closely observed throughout. By Inspector Noguchi, over there.' Otani indicated Noguchi, who had himself seized a pick-axe and was lending a hand with the job of levering up the lumps of concrete broken up by the drills. 'And by

Inspector Hara, head of our criminal investigation section. May I now introduce Mr Hara to you.'

Having been warned about the prosecutor beforehand, Hara was at his punctilious and pedantic best and Akamatsu's frosty manner thawed perceptibly. 'Well done, Hara,' Otani muttered into his ear, having drawn him to one side when the power shovel roared into action to shift the rubble well away from the drilled area, and general conversation became impossible for a few minutes. 'Stick with him, would you? Blind him with procedural science, but don't for heavens sake tell him why we know exactly where to look. He'll have to be satisfied with the usual "acting on information received" formula.'

Hara nodded, rather haughtily Otani thought, and moved back to the prosecutor's side. After a few minutes the layer of concrete had now been cleared away from a roughly square area some twelve feet by twelve, and two labourers tidied up the exposed earth surface with shovels.

'May we now proceed with the digging, Mr Prosecutor?'

'Since that is the object of staging this extremely expensive exercise at such an early hour, you may, yes.'

This time it was the representatives of the forces of law and order who admired the skill of the operator of the power shovel, who knew perfectly well why he had been instructed to excavate to a depth of precisely 1.70 metres and not a centimetre deeper. He also knew the reason why, when this had been done, he and all the other workers employed by the company including the site manager were banished from the scene, leaving only three men in protective overalls behind. These were Noguchi and two beefy detectives from Hara's section, who now swiftly erected a canvas screen round the hole, leaving room for the prosecutor, Otani, Hara and Araki the archaeologist to witness the proceedings from the far side, opposite the mound of earth gouged out and deposited by the power shovel.

Noguchi clambered down into the hole with them, but

sensibly let the two young men do most of the work of digging. Nobody spoke, and the occasional grunt, the sound of their spades and the thumping of the earth they threw up and out on to the pile seemed to accentuate the silence that had all at once descended over the whole of the huge Kobe Royal Heights site.

After a tense few minutes Noguchi signalled the diggers to stop, bent forward, and then beckoned to Otani. He in turn peered into the pit and then turned to Akamatsu.

'It's as we thought, Mr Prosecutor,' he said. 'Inspector Hara, you have your radio with you, I believe. Please summon the scene of crime team. Also arrange for Zenji Ono to be pulled in. An ambulance will be needed here later, of course.' He nodded to the two sweating detectives. 'Thank you, well done both of you. Inspector Noguchi, gently does it, but if sufficient earth could be cleared away for the District Prosecutor to satisfy himself that . . . wherever has he got to?'

*

Pale, and dabbing alternately at his mouth and at his forehead on which beads of sweat kept appearing, the prosecutor reappeared a little later. Otani left it to Hara to lead him to the edge of the pit. Later Otani swore to Hanae that Akamatsu had kept his eyes tightly closed throughout, but he did incline his head as though looking down at the earthly remains of Keizo Hosoda for a second or two before nodding his head violently and then turning his back on the grisly sight.

'You won't have any bother with him after this,' Noguchi said comfortably after Hara, at Otani's request, had escorted a notably less poised prosecutor away to find him a restorative cup of coffee and transport back to his office. Then he turned his head slightly to look to one side. 'What's the matter with that loony?' he then enquired, jerking a thumb towards Mr Araki, about whom Otani had quite forgotten. 'He's been rooting about up there for the last ten minutes.'

Araki was squatting halfway up the mound of excavated earth, seemingly oblivious to the fact that if he were to slip he would undoubtedly tumble straight on to what was left of the late Hosoda. He was fondling what looked like a rotting length of wood, and making little yipping noises.

'Do be careful, Mr Araki!' Otani called. 'What have you got there? Give him a hand, one of you, would you?'

Leaning on the brawny arm of one of the detectives and still tenderly holding the unprepossessing object in his free hand, Araki managed to clamber down to safety and walk round the pit to where Otani and Noguchi were standing. Otani saw that there were tears in his eyes.

'I'm sorry we had to subject you to such a distressing experience, Mr Araki.'

Araki glanced briefly into the pit. 'What, that?' he said. 'Oh, that doesn't bother me.' Then he gazed fervently into Otani's eyes. 'My dear Superintendent, this is the happiest day of my life!'

'It is?'

'Oh yes, yes. He *was* right, you see. Dare I say, even, *we* – he and I – were right. Look at it, isn't it lovely? It must be wrapped at once in plastic to stop the air getting at it before being handed over to the experts for cleaning and treatment, but just a quick peep first, perhaps.' He brandished his find.

'What is it?'

'A sword blade, sir! And if I'm not much mistaken, one dating from Heian times at the latest. Possibly even earlier. Over a thousand years old, conceivably!' He stared hungrily over at the mound of earth, obviously longing to get at it again. 'Dear dear, so much to do, telephone calls to make – you will have this site guarded until I can organise everything, won't you? Who can imagine what other treasurers we may find? It's all so *exciting*!' Araki blinked repeatedly, and wiped his eyes with the back of his free hand. Then his very ordinary features were all at once transfigured by a smile of great tenderness and beauty.

'One thing is quite certain, though,' he said. 'This object is from henceforth to be known as the Kido Sword. In his honour, and in his memory.'